**UNIVERSITY OF GLAMORGAN
LEARNING RESOURCES CENTRE**

Pontypridd, Mid Glamorgan, CF37 1DL
Telephone: Pontypridd (0443) 480480

Books are to be returned on or before the last date below

**General Editor: Aidan Chambers**

THE NATURE OF THE BEAST

# The NATURE of the BEAST

Janni Howker

*m*
*books*

Nelson

Thomas Nelson and Sons Ltd
Nelson House  Mayfield Road
Walton-on-Thames  Surrey
KT12 5PL  UK

Nelson Blackie
Wester Cleddens Road
Bishopbriggs
Glasgow  G64 2NZ  UK

Thomas Nelson (Hong Kong) Ltd
Toppan Building 10/F
22A Westlands Road
Quarry Bay  Hong Kong

Thomas Nelson Australia
102 Dodds Street
South Melbourne
Victoria 3205  Australia

Nelson Canada
1120 Birchmount Road
Scarborough  Ontario
M1K 5G4  Canada

© Janni Howker 1985

First published by Julia McRae Books 1985
First published by Macmillan Education Ltd 1987
ISBN 0-333-413741

This edition published by Thomas Nelson and Sons Ltd 1992

I(T)P  Thomas Nelson is an International
Thomson Publishing Company.

I(T)P  is used under licence.

ISBN 0-17-432492-8
NPN  9 8 7 6 5 4

Printed in Singapore

*For Ian*

# Chapter 1

JOBS BLOW FOR HAVERSTON
Hope for Stone Cross
DOUBLE TRAGEDY FOR LOCAL FARMER
THE HAVERSTON BEAST STRIKES AGAIN!
REWARD OFFERED FOR
HAVERSTON BEAST Beast's Last
Victim

Oh, I remember the headlines, but they don't tell the whole story – newspapers never do. They don't know the half of it. Not one half! And even if they did, I reckon they wouldn't care – not about Dad or Chunder, or the trouble I'm in.

I'll give them headlines! I'll hammer them with headlines until I make this town squint! But I bet you a pound to a pinch of salt that they still won't see the thread. No, they'll not see that all these things are connected up, just like knots in a length of thread . . .

And here's me, Bill Coward, Ned Coward's son and Chunder's grandson – nobody. Nowt. And I'm the only one who really knows about the Beast. But they'll never listen. Maybe you'll not listen either, but I'm telling you it started on that cold January evening when Dad came home from work.

He wasn't walking properly. He held onto the edge of the door, and then onto the sideboard, and he walked very very slowly to his chair, as if he was drunk. I thought he was drunk. He had a letter in his hand. That was about six o'clock. Then Chunder came round about an hour later, and Dad had never moved from his chair, and he hadn't touched the mug of tea I'd made for him.

Chunder *was* drunk. He went out into the backyard to pee in the drain – he was that far gone he didn't fancy climbing the stairs to the bathroom. He sat opposite my dad, but not before pulling a screwed-up letter from his pocket and chucking it into the grate. He put his head in his hands and propped his elbows on his bony knees and watched the letter burn. Then he just sat watching the coals burning into red caves and sparks and black soot, and his face was red in the firelight, like a red skull with black eyes. He's very thin in the face is Chunder.

I thought there was some funeral on or something, but I didn't know what I was seeing – just my old man come home from work and Chunder round visiting. Chunder often comes round to watch the telly, especially in winter when there's not much doing on the allotment. Nowt strange in that, except they said nothing, at least not while I was there.

I must have gone out. I can't quite remember what I'd been up to. Something and nothing . . . Wait on . . . I do remember. Me and Mick Dalton were pelting the phone box with snow-balls, well, slushballs. The snow was melted except for lumps by walls and yellow gritty bits. And Mick and me were lobbing handfuls at Angie Thomson in the phone box just to make her mad.

But the thing was – no one made us come in. We could have stayed out all night, we almost did, with our fingers freezing. Nobody yelled for us to come in, nor for any of the other kids.

And there's usually a lot of yelling goes on in Long Moor Lane after seven. (You know, "Bob Eccles, you get inside this minute or I'll break both yer legs!" She's a good line in yelling has Bob Eccles's mam!)

Most folks in our street worked at Stone Cross Mill, men and women. And most houses had a letter in them, but we didn't know that then. We just kept messing about under the street lamps, waiting for someone to yell. But no one did! It was like everyone had died in their houses and, in the end, it was the silence that took us home. That and the cold.

One by one the kids crept in their own front doors, more cautious and scared than if they were expecting a belting. One by one our street emptied, and there were bright stars, hard as nails, over the moor and a kind of silence, like an echo, as the pavement was left deserted around midnight by kids who were usually murdered if they weren't in by nine . . .

Well, Mick was going slowly round and round the lamp-post, hanging on with one hand, and he says, "What do you reckon's to do?"

"Dunno." I looked at my front door. Number 17.

"Perhaps there's a war," said Mick, and he skidded to a halt.

"Don't be daft."

Mick looked at his front door. Number 23. "See you tomorrow then," he said, but he didn't go.

"If it's a war, we'd know," I said.

And Mick thought a bit, staring at the wet black pavement, his face all in shadows and the back of his head orange with the street light. "Not if it was a secret war. We wouldn't know if it were a secret war."

That's typical Mick, that is!

"Ah, give over! Tarra!" It was too cold and too eerie to hang about. I went in, and I heard the clatter of Mick's footsteps running off down the street behind me.

Chunder was asleep on the sofa, with a can of Harp dangling from his hand and a string of spittle between his lips.

"What's to do, Dad?" I said.

"Get to bed," said Dad.

"But . . . "

"Get!" said Dad.

I went.

I've a slow burning temper, the long-fused kind, Dad says, but with him and Chunder it's light the blue touch-paper and retire. Chunder's the worst. He can swat a wasp with his tongue if he's that way out.

Dad says I get that slow burning from my mam. He says it's the only thing I inherited from her, and it's dangerous and he wishes I hadn't. You see, they only set a long fuse to light a real explosion – like a case of dynamite. The sort of explosion that blows your right leg to Preston and your left leg to Wigan Pier. Or, as in Mam's case, left me on Long Moor Lane, and blew her to Canada.

The blue touch-paper brigade seem more scary at first. A lot of sparks and cracks, belts and swearing, but it's quickly passed over and usually there's no harm done.

Mind you, my great-great-grandad, Snowy Coward, was a blue touch-paper man, and got hisself hanged for it. He was a horse-dealer and he married this gypsy woman called Queenie who was in the same line of trade. They had rows and a baby who was my great-grandad (or, to put it another way, Chunder's Dad), then her real husband, another gypsy man, turns up. And Snowy, being a Coward, chucks him out of the window and he lands on his head, dead. Snowy was hanged at Lancaster Castle. The baby was brought up by neighbours and I expect Queenie went back to the gypsies. I'm not sure.

Dad and Chunder don't really like me talking about this – having a streak of gypsy blood. But you can see it, especially in my dad. He's got black curly hair, and blue eyes that go black when he loses his rag, but just before he goes mad, his eyes go sort of milky, calm and milky. I expect that's what Snowy Coward's eyes were like when he chucked that gypsy feller out of the window.

People say that I'm the spitting image of my dad and a chip off the old block.

While I'm on about family history, I'd better tell you about my mam. I'd have to tell you sometime, so it may as well be now.

My mam and dad weren't married when they had me. They were going to be, then three weeks before the service my mam looks in my cot, and says, "I'm not going to marry you, Ned Coward."

"Why not?" says Dad.

"Me name's Anne. If I married you my name would be A. Coward."

"That's not a reason," says Dad. "You've got to marry us, Annie. That's my lad. It is my lad, isn't it?"

"Oh yes," says Mam. "He's yours all right. And I was a coward to think of marrying you just because of him."

"Me name may be Coward, but there's never been a Coward run away from his kin!"

"That may be," says Mam. "But I'm not a Coward. I'm off. You want him, you keep him."

And she left the house and never came back. Not once. Never. Three weeks later she was in Canada. And a year after that she got married to some bloke. I don't know where she lives. I don't think about her often. But what I've told you is the exact words she spoke, just as Dad told them to me. He was that surprised he didn't have a chance to lose his temper, though he's made up for it since.

Anyway, that's why I was brought up by Dad and Chunder on Long Moor Lane, although they lived in separate rented houses. Sometimes I stayed at Number 3 – which was Chunder's house right on the edge of the moor, and last but one house in Haverston. And sometimes I stayed at Number 17, with Dad, until I was eight and old enough to fend for myself. I've lived with Dad ever since.

Well, anyway, to get back to January. The next morning there were some sparks flying round our kitchen. (There usually are sparks if Dad and Chunder spend more than a couple of hours together, which is why they decided to live in separate houses in the first place, to stop themselves falling out every five minutes.) Chunder had spent the night on the sofa. His clothes were all crumpled and his chin was covered with white bristles, and there was a smell on the room of fag ends, stale beer, leather and sweat. It was the smell of Chunder's house and he had brought it with him.

Dad was cursing Chunder for letting the fire go out. It gets very cold in our house in January, even with the fire in. And it was a thin grey morning. The rain was blowing against the window and it was so dark that we had the light on in the kitchen. The cloud was that low and thick over the valley that you couldn't see the rest of Haverston, not even the chimney of Stone Cross Mill.

"Isn't that flaming kettle boiled yet?" yelled Dad, when I came down.

"Nearly," I said, and went and put it on. I stayed over by the gas cooker because it was the warmest place, and to keep out of the way of them fighting.

"You could have just put a shovel of coal on before you went to sleep!" says Dad, and he's angrily raking and rattling and poking at the fire, getting soot and clinker all over the rug. "You feckless old bugger!"

"Feckless! I'll give thee flaming feckless!" Chunder shouts back, yanking at a knot in his shoe-lace. "Baah! I don't know why I bother wi' thee and tha brat. I shoulda washed me hands of thee! Tha's that self-righteous tha'd sleep in thee Sunday boots!"

"And yer that sodding idle you'd sooner sleep int' grate

than set yer loafing carcase in a bed!"

"It'd be a damn sight warmer if I did! It's a cold welcome in a cold house is all I ever get from thee, Ned Coward. I'd be warmer in me flaming grave!"

This went on. I made a pot of tea and got the bacon out of the cupboard. This was normal with Dad and Chunder. Cowards can fight Cowards, but there's closed ranks and thief-thick blue bloody murder if an outsider says owt against them.

At least, I thought it was normal, until suddenly Chunder looks out into the dark rainy morning and stops silent in the middle of what he's yelling. Then he says, terrible quiet, "Ned? Ned? I can't see t'chimney . . . "

I could have told him that, but Dad goes quiet as well. "Neither can I," he says, and he goes over and puts his hand on Chunder's shoulder. "But it's still standing yet . . . "

It's so quiet I daren't even light a match to set the frying-pan on, for fear of the loudness of the noise.

"It's only the rain," I say at last, because I'm getting a strange silky feeling in my guts. The silence. The sound of the rain. And them staring out of the window like that. "It's only a cloud over the valley," I say.

"It's a blacker bloody cloud than you've mind of," says Dad, quietly.

Chunder nodded. Looking at them, I got the feeling that the weight of my dad's hand on Chunder's shoulder was making my grandad stoop, and then I looked at my dad's back, and it was as if an even heavier invisible hand was pressing down on his shoulders, making him hunched and bowed. That silky feeling in my belly got worse. I forgot about the bacon and went and stood next to my dad — for a very long time, it seemed.

It's strange now, looking back. I can see a picture in my mind of all the windows of the terraced houses on Long Moor Lane on that dark morning, with the moor behind. And at the yellow squares of glass, people are standing. All silent. Whole families. Standing and gazing down at the valley, with their breath steaming up the cold glass, looking for Stone Cross Mill chimney in that smoky cloud, and for the first time in their lives, fearing that it wouldn't be there.

I didn't know what I was looking at. Only that I was peering into the valley as if my life depended on it.

Then Dad straightened his back.

Chunder said, "What time's Jim Dalton called that meeting for?"

(Jim Dalton is my mate's – Mick Dalton's – dad. He was the shop steward.)

"Eleven. In the car park."

"Eleven," repeated Chunder. He went over to the table and poured himself a mug of tea, and he looked for a long time at the teapot. "I'll not go, Ned," he said, after a while, "I'm too old to hear that noise."

"What about your vote?" said Dad, without looking round.

"Vote?" says Chunder. "Me vote won't make a tinker's cuss of difference." And he drank his tea all the way to the leaves without remembering that he'd forgotten to put sugar in. That gave me a shock. Chunder drinking tea without sugar, and not even noticing! He's a sweet tooth, has Chunder.

"What's to do, Dad?" I said.

"Get to school!" said Dad.

Mick said, "Well, are we bunking off or what?"

He was scratching something into the green paint of the bus shelter. Above it, someone had scratched MOOR MODS ROOL OK – which is stupid, because there's no such thing as real Mods round here any more. I expect they just liked the sound of it.

"Looks like we are," I said, because the bus had gone. Then I said, "What's happening?"

"That's just what I asked!" said Mick, making his eyes all dramatic and exasperated like Oggy. (Oggy – Mr Oglethorpe – is our form master. He also teaches us history and English since Mrs Clegg went off to have a baby.)

I crouched down on my heels, wedged in the corner of the bus shelter. It smelled a bit like Chunder's house down there. All the slush and snow had gone. All the cleanness and coldness of the winter had gone. Today, everything was grey and chilly and bleak. "No, I mean . . . is it a strike your old feller's calling?"

"No," said Mick. "Didn't your dad say?"

"No."

"Oh . . . " There was a bit of silence.

"WELL?"

"They're closing Stone Cross. Making the work-force repugnant."

"Repugnant?"

"Redundant – repugnant. It was me dad's joke – sort of joke. He wants them to accept the terms."

"Closing Stone Cross!" I couldn't believe it. Then I saw what he was scratching into the paint.

Stone Cross
R.I.P

and the date.

"And your dad says yes!"

Mick shrugged. "It's done. There's nowt to say yes or no about, except the settlements."

"They'll kill him," I said to myself.

"That's what I said," said Mick. His voice went odd, whiny and scratchy. He was my best mate, but at that moment I thought I hated him, because he looked frightened, and because his dad was meant to be the union and had let them close Stone Cross.

Then the next moment it was me that was afraid. A sort of blue rippling fear in my belly. Stone Cross chimney was like a church spire in West Haverston. It was like seeing a church spire demolished by lightning; and Chunder and Dad, they were like the congregation standing with their shoulders hunched, waiting for the mortar and bricks to land on them. A hundred tons of bricks on each shoulder, enough to crush every bone in their chests.

For a moment even thinking about it was like spitting splintered bones.

"Don't be daft! They'd not close Stone Cross! Not sudden. Not like that!"

No answer.

"Chunder's worked there since he was thirteen! He's only got two more years to do. Cowards don't go on the dole, Dad says. Cowards don't go on the dole!"

"Do you know what my dad says?" hissed Mick, suddenly fierce. "Do you?"

I shook my head.

Mick was still scratching the paint with the stone. Not writing, but scratching. Screek-screek-screek. "He says he's been fighting a losing battle. He says he's spent eight years trying to wake up Stone Cross shop-floor. Now they've got what they had coming to them – and serves them bloody well right!"

"I don't get it," I said. It was that cold and wet in the bus shelter I began to shiver. Haverston. Our town. Stone Cross chimney. And a thin bitter wind off the moor. The last bus gone. I looked at Mick.

"He says he's been warning them for two years it was coming, but they'd not believe him. He says they think Stone Cross is holy untouchable blooming sanctuary. He says he's seen more pigs fly than pickets from Haverston."

"There must have been a lot of talking in your house this morning," I said.

"This morning!" Mick made a noise in his mouth. "They talked all night!"

"Come on," I said. "Let's go up the allotments. We can sit in Chunder's shed."

So that's where we went, threading our way through the scruffy old corrugated iron and the tatty planks and bits of formica, and last year's dead leaves, until we came to Chunder's patch, which is the last one and the biggest because it's next to the moor. Every year Chunder digs a bit further into the moor, moves his fence a few feet further up the slope. Puts more hens on. The C.E.C. Reclamation Scheme, he calls it. (C.E.C. stands for Charles Ernest Coward.)

Chunder's shed is all made of old doors, all painted red, and the numbers are still on them, and he's painted the numbers very neatly in yellow. The hen house is made of doors as well and painted just the same. It always reminds me of dodgems and fair-grounds for some reason, and I think it might be something to do with the gypsy in Chunder that he paints things like that. Even the handles of shovels and forks and that are painted. He collects the doors from skips and demolitions and there's always a few stacked by the shed, ready to be turned into something or other.

It's dark in the shed, and smells of soil and tar and fag ends and chicken feed.

We sat on some sacks and left the door open so we could watch the rain and so we could watch the daft way the hens kept scurrying out of their coop and nipping back in again, shaking their bum-feathers with annoyance at getting wet. We might have laughed at that if we'd been in a different mood. Instead, we just crouched there, smoking. I'd found a packet with eight fags in, that Chunder must have left last time he was up, and I still had the matches in my pocket from forgetting to set the bacon on. And because the day was so wet and grey, the smoke hung in the shed in coils and layers.

I crouched on my heels, cupping the fag in my hand and watching the blue smoke snake and ribbon between my fingers. It stains your fingers if you hold a fag like that, but I just wanted to watch the smoke, and not think about anything, until my eyes and my thinking were full of these cool blue coils of smoke and I'd almost forgotten that Mick was there.

Then he said, "What will your dad do?"

"Kill the buggers," I said, without thinking. And then I thought of Snowy Coward, and my heart gave this one cold jerk. But that was daft, really daft.

Dad would do what Chunder was already doing – get drunk, swear, shout, fall into bed with his clothes on and I'd have to undress him and cover him with a blanket so as he didn't catch cold. And the next morning he'd be in a worse temper because he'd have a thick head, and I'd keep out of his way. And the morning after that, we'd manage.

"I dunno," I said. "He'll do something. Chunder was going to get pensioned off soon anyway. He's got these plans for his allotment – breeding these special kind of hens." I glanced at Mick.

Mick pulled a face, half grinning and half disgusted, sharing in the secret. Chunder was planning to breed fighting-cocks. It's not illegal to breed them, only to fight them. I'll just say that Chunder was planning to breed them. They're worth a lot of cash to the right blokes.

Mick doesn't approve of anything like that, blood sports and that, and his mother belongs to this anti-foxhunting group. No, she doesn't approve of blood sports, and she doesn't approve of Cowards neither, which is one reason, I reckon, that Mick and me are best mates. She and his dad are very Socialist. They wouldn't even let Mick play with toy guns when he was a little kid, so when we were at junior school he used to come round my house and use my air-rifle instead.

He'd stalk sparrows like he was the SAS and blast away at them. He wasn't a very good shot because he never practised with cans, and half the time he'd miss. And sometimes he'd wing starlings or blackbirds and then I'd have to kill them, wring their necks, because he couldn't bring himself to do it. I couldn't see the point. You can't eat sparrows and that – well, you can, but there's not much point. I'd rather shoot at tin cans and the occasional rabbit and pigeon for Chunder to make a pie. But Mick used to go mad with my air-rifle. He even scared me sometimes.

He doesn't shoot sparrows now, and he's got very righteous about things like that. But I still think that secretly he wants to. Just every now and again you can see this grin on his mouth, a tiny, nasty smile. Like when we were doing about the Nazis and the Jews, and he kept trying to get Oggy to tell us in detail what exactly they did to the Jews. He was very righteous about it. He said we had a right and a need to know just what it was the Allies were fighting against. But I could see that grin on his mouth, just at the corners. I think he enjoyed hearing about that cruelty, but he'd kill me if I ever let on that that was what I thought.

I don't mean to say that he's a pervert or anything. He's my best mate, and I've seen that look on other people's faces as well, like when they're reading about a murder in the newspaper, lapping up the gory details. It's the same sort of look as they get when they read about sex, I think. Maybe I get that sort of look when I read about sex. I don't know.

Anyway, we spent this pretty miserable day in Chunder's shed, not talking much, just smoking our heads off. Well you can't really smoke your head off with eight fags, I suppose, but neither Mick nor me are great smokers. I'm not bothered one way or the other, and I shan't smoke when I grow up. But we were that fed up we smoked the lot. The only real talking we did was when I told Mick about my Plan.

My Plan had been a secret and a day-dream until then. I

hadn't even told Mick before, but we were talking about West Haverston ending up like East Haverston where everyone is ending up on the dole. And I told Mick that I was never going to go up on the dole, because I had a Plan. And the Plan is this – that I take my air-rifle and some other things, not a lot, but a very useful list, and go up on the moors and live in a cave, and eat rabbits and grouse and seagulls. And I'll get a couple of lurchers; maybe a ferret. I'm not sure about the ferret yet. And I'll just live as I like, like a gypsy, like a wild man on the moors, where they can't grind you down.

If it gets a bit bad in winters I'll maybe have to sneak into the towns and raid the allotments and that. Not bad thieving, just getting enough to eat and drink. A couple of milk bottles off early morning doorsteps, even eggs when the milkman delivers the eggs as well, and the fruit and vegetables that are left scattered about Garden Street on a Wednesday evening after the street market.

I don't mean I want to be a tramp, just a sort of free wild man up on the moors.

Well, we talked for a long time about that, and it made us feel a lot better, as if we were actually planning to do it. And Mick came up with one or two suggestions – like you could pinch the occasional shirt and pair of jeans off washing-lines. Never from the same house twice, because that wouldn't be fair, especially if the people were poor. In fact, we'd probably pinch them off Laurel Ridge private housing estate, because you get a better class of jeans up there, Levis and Wranglers and that. And because the people are mostly rich on Laurel Ridge.

And then he had this idea about us becoming kind of modern highwaymen in the summer, when there are tourists about on the moors. (Mick had it in his head by then that we'd do the Plan together. I didn't tell him that I would only ever go alone, even though he is my best mate. He'd be pretty feckless when it came to the crunch. And, also, he'd land us in trouble, like his suggestion about being highwaymen proves.)

He reckoned that to be highwaymen we'd need an old motorbike, and what we'd do is lie the bike on the road and one of us would sprawl under or near it, with some tomato sauce on their face, so that it looked like a really bad accident, and the other one would flag down a car. And then, when the people got out and came rushing to help, we'd hold them up with the air-rifle and rob them of their money and useful gear! I reckon it's a pretty mean thing to do, and it would only possibly work once. But it's just the sort of thing Mick dreams up!

It wasn't part of my Plan at all, but Mick got really excited and I had to watch him practise playing dead, sprawling on the shed floor as if he'd had a terrible accident, and make daft comments like, "You'll have to hold your breath for longer than that." Or, "Try and make your leg look more crooked, like it was really broken."

It was fun in a way, and it stopped us thinking about Stone Cross. And then it got even funnier when Mick was pretending to hold up this really rich tourist and saying, "Your money or your wife?"

And I said in an American accent, "Ah, to hell with it! Take ma wife!"

We just fell about laughing at that. It doesn't sound very funny when you tell it afterwards but things like that are really funny when they happen on the spur of the moment.

Then we could hear kids yelling on the streets, and we were both hungry, so we went home.

Chunder was in at Number 17 but Dad wasn't. As soon as I walked in the door the silky feeling came back, and the laughing went away. I asked so many whys and that many hows about the Mill closing that in the end Chunder lost his rag.

"It's just the nature of the bloody beast, Billy! It's just the nature of the bloody beast!" he yelled.

And the silken balloon in my gut swelled up and pressed on my lungs. I lay in bed that night. It was still raining. Dad didn't come home. Half the men and women on Long Moor Lane didn't come home – except Mick's dad. But no one would have recognised him because he came home looking and walking like Mick's grandad, and he never went out again for a week.

The rest of Long Moor Lane was occupying Stone Cross. For all the good it did.

That was the night Chunder came to live with us. Nothing official. He just moved in. He never moved out again. He brought no luggage, but over the next few weeks his bits and pieces found space in our house. As Number 3 emptied, Number 17 filled. If nothing else, it made Number 17 look more homely, and it made the house smell different.

It was pretty daft when you think about it – Chunder and Dad both paying rent and living next to each other.

All Chunder said was, "Looks like tha dad won't be in this night. Best I stay wi' thee, lad."

"Aye. Best you stay, Chunder," I said, because I could tell that he didn't want to be by himself. I made him a bacon butty and he went round the off-licence for a couple of cans, and then we watched the news.

Seven hundred jobs to go in the textile industry. Picture of Stone Cross chimney, red and towering like a cathedral against a blue sky.

That's too much for Chunder. "They've known all along!" he yells. "That picture were never taken this month! That's summer, that is! Some blighter's known since last flaming summer!"

Last summer, when Fred Dibnah climbed his ladders to the top and scared the kestrels off their nest, making them scream, "Kree-kree". It's there on the screen, and Chunder's yelling in this chopped up voice like someone's hitting him in the throat.

"Grandad! Chunder!" I yell back, though he's sitting right beside me. "Don't be daft. That's the picture they took when Fred Dibnah was doing the repointing job. It must have been the only picture they had."

Chunder settles down a bit then. "Oh," he said. "Oh aye. Bloody good job he made of it an' all. Grand job. Champion job. Watched him put linseed in the mortar . . . Champion job . . . It'll last another hundred years that mortar int' chimney . . . "

If I said Chunder was crying then I'd be lying to you. But he was crying in a way. Not with tears in his eyes, but just like splinters of bone were stuck in his throat.

"Best flaming steeplejack this side of the Pennines, is Fred," said Chunder.

I switched off the telly.

On the news it wasn't real. But when the screen went grey and blank, then it was real. Stone Cross Mill was closing. Dad and Chunder were being made redundant. There's no more jobs in Haverston to go to. First they closed down Hallingfords, then the biscuit factory, then the brewery, then Haverston Rubber Company and Langley's . . .

I don't know why, but Chunder and me went and sat on the stairs in the dark and the cold. Perhaps it was to get away from the telly. We sat very silent, with the smell of the beer and the house and the coal smoke blowing back down the chimney, and the patter of rain against the front door. And that feeling, like a silky blue flame, burning very slowly, was still there.

After a time, Chunder starts humming softly to himself, and singing snatches,

> "I am a roving jack
> A roving jack of all trades
> And if you want te-tum te-tum
> You can call me Jack of all trades . . . "

But he doesn't sing all the words, although I know he knows all the words, and he hardly bothers with the tune. He just sings the odd te-tum and Jack of all trades and up and down the country in the dark hallway. And he hums and sings very softly, so it's almost as if there's a ghost on the landing that's singing as it passes through the walls, and it doesn't sound like Chunder at all.

Now, usually, if Chunder's got the singing mood on him, it means that he's in right good fettle, and the next thing is that he'll tell you some story about the olden days, because the song will have reminded him of something. But not that night. That night it was like the ghost of Chunder Coward singing in the rainy dark.

We stayed there for a long time, then I went to bed.

"Night, Chunder," I said.

His thin shadow stood in the doorway against the landing light.

"Don't get drunk," I said.

"The fire's set," said Chunder. "Night, lad. Eh, I could drink Lancashire dry – soberly, mind. Drink it dry, soberly. Sober as signing me own death warrant, our Bill."

"Yer drunk, Chunder," I whispered.

"Drunk dry," said my grandad. "Drunk dry and cold as a bloody desert."

I heard him creak downstairs, then the whispery click of him peeling open the ring-pull on another can.

I couldn't sleep. I wasn't angry or scared or owt. I wasn't in any mood that I could easily put a name to. It was like waiting, perhaps. Like waiting to be afraid and angry. I wonder some times if that's what those soldiers in Belfast feel when they're kneeling on street corners with a gun on routine patrol. Waiting, like that.

In the end I got out of bed and went to the window. The rain was still crying down the glass, and Haverston was quiet under a yellowish cloud, with the dark night over the Pennines and the yellow street-lamps below. I stood there, cold, listening to the wind off the night moors. And maybe something else was listening. Something that kills hens and sheep and sometimes men . . . Something that hears you, and comes closer . . .

No. No. It wasn't like that. That's the thread. I only went to the window to see if my dad was coming home in time to pick up some fish and chips from Danny's. But the chip shop light was out. It was dark. I stood looking into the dark.

# Chapter 2

Next day, Mick wasn't at the bus stop and he wasn't at school neither, but I decided to go anyway. Mind you, I can't blame him, because overnight the name of Dalton had turned to mud, with folks saying that if his dad had talked more sense and less politics things might be very different at Stone Cross. And even though Mick had started doing karate, that wouldn't have saved him. (His mam has the weird idea that karate is something to do with peace and self-control, but Mick thinks it's about being able to kick someone in the crotch faster than lightning!)

Although every one knows that Mick's my mate, they didn't bother me. I'm not right sure why. Maybe it's because I didn't bother them, or maybe, just maybe, it's because Cowards have a bit of a reputation. It's not my reputation like, it's Dad's and Chunder's for flying off the handle. I've only ever lost my rag twice at school. Mind you, the last time I broke my arm trying to kill Fats Grundy. He was a slobby sixth former. And, I swear, I was trying to kill him. I'm not proud of that. It scared me to death when I woke up and found Oggy sitting on my chest, with blood all over his shirt (my blood) because I couldn't remember who I'd been trying to kill, or why. And for an instant I thought it must have been Oggy. Anyway, it wasn't. And I didn't. And Fats Grundy had made a better job of killing me than I had of him. Oggy took me to hospital.

Anyway, I was telling you about the next day . . . I went into our class room, and Oggy says, "Had a nice holiday, Coward?"

And I say, "Yes thanks, Sir."

And he says, "Send us a postcard next time. Have you done that homework? Or need I ask?"

And I say, "What homework, Sir?"

And he says, "Oh never mind, Coward. Sit down. Not at the back!"

And I say, "But that's where I sit, Sir. That's me desk."

And he says, "Ah, what the hell." Which is one of the things he often says to me. And the other thing he says, sometimes, is, "You're a dark horse, Coward." That's when I do hand in homework, when it's something I'm interested in.

Oggy teaches history, and we did this thing once, called an Oral History project, and I did about Chunder. All I did was write down everything he told me about the great General Strike of 1926, and how he and Nodder Smith had taken a cart up onto the moors and dug peat and made a packet, because there was no coal to be had because of the strike, and everyone wanted to buy the peat to cook and keep warm. And how, also, they'd struck this deal with one of the Boswells – I shan't say which one because he's still alive for all I know – about him supplying poached salmon and trout for them to sell to the local hotels. (When I say poached, I don't mean cooked like poached eggs – I mean nicked out of a private river with a gaff hook or nets and a torch, and once, with gunpowder. BOOM-KERSPLOSH! Fish everywhere! Floating, bellies up!) And how all this happened when Chunder was on strike from Stone Cross, and how he almost didn't go back to work when the strike was over because he had made more money being on strike than being at work.

I got a prize for that project. It wasn't much of a prize. A book token. I swapped it with Mick for the cash, and he sold it to his dad. But after that and the broken arm, Oggy often says to me, "What the hell," and "You're a dark horse, Coward," and we get on all right.

Mostly I don't like teachers much. I'll tell you why and all.

It's because they make out they know all these things, but they only know them because they've been told by someone else, or read it in a book. It's not like they've done it for themselves. Oggy isn't quite like that – even though he teaches history. He goes and digs history up. He once found a Roman sword. I'm not lying. He dug it up and it's in Haverston Municipal Museum. It doesn't look like much – just like a thin small rusty crow-bar. But it is a real Roman sword.

Some of the other teachers don't like him because he swears and threatens to knee-cap kids who don't do what he says, and he spends half the time telling stories. Some of the other teachers reckon he shouldn't be telling stories about what it was like when his dad was with Rommel and Monty in the desert, and how Monty was like a puffy little runt when you first saw him, but you soon learned he was deadly as a snake. They don't reckon that's history, but I do. It's like the stories Chunder tells.

And, another thing I like about Oggy, is that he doesn't try to be friendly. Like, we have this other teacher that we call Twanger Harrison, but he's always wanting us to call him Dave. He's supposed to teach maths, but he belongs to this group, and he's always asking us what kind of music we like and that. A lot of the girls like him, because he plays an electric guitar and has an ear-ring in one ear (at least, he did have until the Head noticed). But he's the sort I hate most. He's just trying to be all friendly because he's scared of us, and because he's decided that we're too thick to learn maths. I hate him, and he hates me, although I've never said a word in class. And he always calls me Will, not Coward, not even Bill. All I ever did to him was once I put my feet up on the desk, just stretched out and comfy, while he nattered on – just to see what he'd do. He'd made out that he was so cool and friendly, but he was itching to come and break both my legs, you could see. Because of all the things he'd made himself out to be, he didn't even dare tell me to take my boots off the desk!

And afterwards, at the end of the class, he called me to his desk, and he was sitting there with his lanky knees and legs dangling down, and he says, "Will – uh – look, I'm really interested in the Romanies." (That means like gypsies.) "Do you speak Romany yourself? I mean – uh – it's really very interesting . . . " Never a word about my feet.

"I'm not a flaming gypsy!" I said. I didn't mean anything against the Romanies or any of the travelling people. I just hated what he was trying to do. Standing next to him was like catching a disease. Then I walked out. Sometimes I go to maths now. Sometimes I don't.

Wait on. Wait on. This is giving you the wrong idea. Daft as it might sound, mostly I like school, and mostly I don't like trouble. Mostly I sit quiet and listen, and, if it's interesting, I do some writing down. Sometimes I even get B's, and sometimes I get prizes. (Well, twice.) The teachers that know me leave me alone, but the new ones and the students get on my back.

Anyway, that day passes. And some more days pass. I haven't seen my old man, and Chunder's mostly drunk, and Mick isn't around. And it's still raining.

I'm getting a bit fed up of emptying Chunder's ash-trays and making him beefburgers and chips and bacon butties and feeding his hens. I want to see my dad. Then one tea-time Chunder comes in, grinning all over his face, waving a letter.

"What is it?" I said.

"It's a letter, Billy. It's a letter!"

"I can see that!"

"Eh, but you'll never guess what's in it, our Bill!" says Chunder, dropping his cap on the table and pulling a four-pack out of his coat pocket. "Everyone's got one!"

"Oh, well you can't have won the pools then."

"No, you daft youth! Allt' folks occupying Stone Cross. It's a letter from the bosses, Bill, says here, like, for them to go home and we'll all think about the future for a week. Negotiations, Billy. Negotiations . . . "

"Grand," I says. "Does that mean Dad'll be home!"

"I reckon it does. We've got bosses on the run. We'll have 'em eating out of our hands in no time. You mark my words, lad."

I turned on the telly, and would you believe it? There's my dad, on the news, for less than a second. He's standing in a window at Stone Cross Mill, but his eyes are milky. And he's listening to all the things that the TV people are saying into the cameras, and watching all the people from Stone Cross who are grinning like idiots and waving at their Aunty Maud because it's the first time they've been on telly. But all I see, for less than a split second, is my dad's face, full of black lines, and his eyes. And I ran.

I ran to get him and stop him. I didn't know what he was going to do, but when Dad looks like that it means trouble. And what Snowy Coward once did is always somewhere at the back of my mind.

Stone Cross Mill chimney is about a mile as the crow flies from our chimney. The top of that chimney and ours look about level, although we're higher up, being on the edge of the moor. Running, it's about a hundred miles. Well, it seems like that. It's about one and a half miles really, but in the dark and the rain, and not knowing if Chunder's going to fall asleep with a can in one hand and a fag in the other that's going to burn the house down, it's a hundred.

It's not far from my school and, only in autumn, the shadow of the chimney lies across the playground for a few weeks. A wide black strip of shadow, and though we all know what it is, none of the little kids will walk through it if they can help it. I didn't when I was a little kid. Only the older kids stand there. The West Haverston kids, lounging like lizards in the sun. Only it isn't the sun, it's shadow, and there aren't any lizards round Haverston, although there are adders up on the moors.

Anyway, I ran and got a stitch, and hopped up to the gates.

Then suddenly it's like bonfire night, because there's this crowd at the gates round a fire, with banners, and everyone's drinking cans of lager and beer, celebrating the new letter. But my dad isn't there.

And it's odd as well. These great long shadows of people walking about on the mill wall. And the thin black stripes of the gate, and the look on the men's faces, as if they were in a film – faces half lit up and half in darkness, watching two panda cars. And the women are there as well, women that work in the mill, and though they're soaked to the skin their faces are bright, like on a Saturday night. But the newsmen ignored them. They wanted faces and eyes like my dad's for their pictures.

I couldn't see him anywhere, and I was wet through and freezing and fed up, wishing I hadn't come.

The police stopped me first. The panda car door opened and this copper grabbed me by the arm. He didn't want to get out of the car because of the rain, but he didn't mind me standing in it.

I just said, "I'm looking for me dad. He asked me to come down with his tea."

Then he let me go. I suppose he must have said something to me – but I don't rightly remember what. I just had to find me dad before he did a Snowy on us.

Suddenly, I hear this voice yelling my name. "Coward!" It's so familiar that I can't place it. It's so familiar and in the wrong setting that everything seems like a dream. I run through the black shadows, past the yellow leaping flames, and under the dripping elbows of the pickets.

"Coward!"

I've never been inside Stone Cross gate before, and the chimney is half lit up and it looks as if it's toppling down on me out of the darkness.

And then, suddenly, there's history repeating itself.

It's Oggy, in the shadows, far away from the camera lights and out of sight of the police, kneeling on my dad's chest.

Oh, there's one thing I've forgotten to tell you about Oggy –

he weighs about sixteen stone and plays rugby for the county, at least he did until last year, when he got this cartilage in his knee that stopped him playing.

You might think that if you saw someone kneeling on your old feller's chest you'd rush up and try and beat the living daylights out of them. The thought never crossed my mind.

I ran in and out of the stripes of shadow until I stood looking down at them. My dad's got his eyes closed and a bit of blood on his mouth, and he's panting, "Uh-uh-uh-uh." I'm surprised he could even breathe with sixteen stones of Oggy on his ribs. And I notice that there's a cob-end of a brick lying near his hand, just out of reach, but I can tell that he has been reaching for it, because of the way his fingers are flexing and curling and trying to creep across the tarmac like a crab.

"What are you doing here, Sir?" I said.

"Came-to-take-some-photos for-the-old-archive . . . " Oggy sort of panted, like. "Oh," I said, "I think yer suffocating me dad, Sir," I said, because now Dad was lying very still and breathing, "Heww-hheww-hhew."

Oggy looked down at my dad's face, then slowly, like an experiment, he relaxed his muscles and let go of Dad's shoulders. Dad didn't move, but I kicked the cob-end away, just in case. Then Oggy got up and stood astride Dad's chest, and I could hear that my old man was still breathing, which was a relief.

"What was to do, Sir?" I said.

Oggy wiped his mouth with his sleeve. "Just a friendly knock about," he said, then he stepped away to where his camera and a black case of camera equipment were lying in a heap in the rain. "Come on, I'll take you home."

"What about me dad?"

"And him, Coward. And him," said Oggy. "Come on, my old son," he says, and sort of hoicks Dad up onto his feet, and puts his arm round Dad's waist, and Dad's arm over his shoulder. I carry the black case and the camera and, just as we set off for the gate, I pick up the cob-end as well and put it in my jacket, in case it's got Dad's fingerprints all over it. By then, you see, I'd noticed the white Mercedes, with the number plate SCM 1, and its windscreen is all bashed in.

Nobody stopped us leaving. I suppose the policeman probably recognised Mr Oglethorpe, because Oggy just said, "Got a sick man here, Derek. His son came to collect him. Nothing serious. I'll run them home."

"Right-ho," says this policeman called Derek, who's only young, and was probably taught by Mr Oglethorpe once upon a time.

I'd never been inside Oggy's car – at least not when I was conscious, because I was unconscious when he took me to the hospital with a broken arm. You would think that with him being a teacher his car would be smart on the inside, but it isn't. It's full of old toffee papers, and bits of newspapers and shoes, and it smells like the changing rooms in the gym.

"Are you all right, Dad?" I said. I was sitting in the back seat with him.

He shook his head – not meaning to say no, just to wake himself up. "Aye."

I could see Oggy glance in the rear-view mirror when we stopped at the traffic lights, but he didn't say anything.

I could smell on my dad's breath that he'd been drinking. In fact he's that drunk, that he starts to sing, "It's not the leaving of Liverpool that grieves me, but my-y dar-ling when I think of yo-ooou . . . " as we turn up the hill towards Long Moor Lane.

"Sir?" I said, and tapped Oggy on the shoulder.

"Shouldn't distract someone when they're driving, Coward," said Oggy.

"I only wanted to say thanks, Sir. For sitting on me dad, and that."

"S'alright," said Oggy. "Forget it, Coward. Forget it, and don't mention it."

"I shan't."

"Good lad." He parked the car outside our house. I don't know why, but it surprised me a bit that he knew exactly where we lived.

"Can you manage, Coward?" he said, and turned off the windscreen wipers. He helped Dad out of the car into the pelting rain, but he didn't come to the door with us – which I was glad about because I didn't want him to for some reason. I don't know why not.

Dad's got his arm round my neck, and he's swaying about, half pulling my head off each time he gets to the chorus of *Maggie-May*, and we're both soaked to the bone. But it's all right now. This is normal, and at least he's standing on his own two feet. (You should have seen him and Chunder at Christmas!)

Mr Oglethorpe gets back in his car and he sits in it, with the lights switched off, and the engine switched off, staring up at our house.

I know he stayed there for quite a while, because I saw him from Dad's bedroom window when I was putting Dad to bed, but he'd gone by the time I got round to stoking up the fire. Chunder was asleep on the sofa, and he hadn't even bothered to fill the coal-bucket. Idle old sod.

It was only when I was in bed that night that I began to go hot and cold with thinking what might have happened if Oggy hadn't turned up and stopped my dad . . . If the police had seen him and tried to stop him . . .

It'll sound soft, but thinking about it like that made me feel very very tired. Not the sort of tired that puts you to sleep, but the sort of tired that makes tears sneak out of your eyes and you can't help it . . .

Mind you, I partly blame whoever left that flashy white Merc there in the first place. I mean, if it hadn't been my old feller who happened to be near when its windscreen just happened to get smashed, someone else would have been there. There was killing in the air by then, and a lot of bad feeling flying about – enough bad feeling flying about to stove in the windscreen of a flashy boss's car like that.

Anyway, that hot and cold feeling didn't go away for the next few days. And I got this pain in my side. It's daft, the things you think when you're ill, but really I thought I'd probably got lung cancer because of smoking those fags in Chunder's shed.

In fact, I didn't know I had a pain at all until about one o'clock the next afternoon. I was still in bed, with this feeling like I couldn't be bothered to wake up properly. Every now and again I could hear Dad roaring from the next room to bring him a cup of tea. "I know you're there, Billy Coward! I can hear yer breathing!" he yelled. Things like that. But I just couldn't be bothered somehow, and although I knew he was shouting, and it was me he was after, partly it seemed like I was dreaming it.

Then he comes stamping into my room with a rug round his shoulders, but no clothes on, so that he looks like an Apache Indian on the war-path. He yanks the sheets and blankets off me, grabs me by the arm and pulls me up.

That's when I found out about the pain. It wasn't there before – then suddenly I heard someone yell out loud, and a second later I knew it was me shrieking, and a second after that I felt the pain, like someone had axed me in the ribs.

Dad let go. He looked pretty awful as well. Then there was a great thumping up the stairs. It was Chunder, shouting, "You leave that lad alone, Ned Coward, or I'll break every bone in your body!" Bless him. The daft devil thought he was rescuing me from a belting.

By then Dad was rubbing his hand gently through my hair, and saying, "What's to do, our Billy? What's to do, lad? I didn't mean to hurt you? Did I hurt your arm or something?"

Well, to cut a long story short, I was ill for the next few days. I don't remember a lot about it, except for when Chunder ties this piece of brown wrapping-paper round my chest, that stinks of fat – goose-grease. Hot goose-grease. I thought he was going to burn my skin off, but he must have got the temperature just right because he didn't burn me, and it did help a bit, even if it did stink like cooking. And he made me drink hot whisky with sugar and lemon in it – which I quite liked.

Apart from the pain, it was almost nice being ill and, besides, it kept Dad away from Stone Cross, which I reckon was a good thing. I've never been ill very much – apart from accidents like the broken arm, and getting bitten by the Eccles's Alsatian when I was seven. It made a change to have Chunder and Dad making me mugs of tea and sausage sandwiches.

Dad kept asking Chunder if he didn't think they should get the quack, but Chunder said it was only a touch of pneumonia and he'd soon have me as right as rain. He fancies himself as a bit of a medicine man, does Chunder. I reckon that's probably the gypsy in him and all.

Dad even fixed up the telly so I could watch it in bed. One night, when the wind was howling off the moor and making our chimney hoot, all three of us were lounging on my bed, watching this horror movie and drinking hot whisky with sugar in it. And, just for a short time, in the middle of all that disaster about Stone Cross, I felt really happy. I suppose it might just have been the whisky and the fact that I was getting better. Maybe it was just that. And maybe it was also the fact that Dad said Oggy had been round to see why I wasn't at school. Dad said that Oggy seemed like an OK bloke. And I said he was. And it was obvious that Dad couldn't remember anything that had happened about the Merc and Oggy sitting on his chest. That pleased me as well, because it made it seem as if it hadn't really ever happened at all.

# Chapter 3

Everyone thought that new letter from Stone Cross was a good thing, and that maybe it meant the bosses had changed their minds and wouldn't close it down after all. The headline in the *Haverston Gazette* that Friday was HOPE FOR STONE CROSS.

On Saturday I was a lot better, so I got up. Chunder went out to see some blokes over at Kirkby Haverston (which is a little village about four miles away on the moors) at a pub called *The Hare and Hounds*, officially, and *The Cocks* by people who know it. And Dad went off down town to meet up with one of the East Lancashire Smiths he was friendly with, on account of the fact that this bloke was in town with a circus that was passing through. And Dad, I reckon, is quite friendly with Dancer Smith's sister.

So I decided to go and see Mick. It was quite hard doing that, because when I got out of bed, the room began to go round very slowly and I almost fell over. It made me laugh a bit did that, because sometimes when my old feller's merry drunk he says, "When that bed comes round again I'll get in it. Aim me in the right direction, Bill!"

Well, I got as far as Number 23. It was bright and cold in the street, and the wind was snapping the washing in the back-yards, and you could see Stone Cross chimney as clear as your own finger stuck up in front of your face.

It was Mick's mam who opened the door. "Oh," says she. "What do you want?"

Now I know that Mrs Dalton doesn't really approve of the Cowards, but I didn't expect that – least ways, not off her. You see, she's not really like any of the other women on Long Moor Lane. She doesn't dress like them for a start – more like the women on Laurel Ridge. I don't mean she's fancy, la-di-da, she just is slim and wears jeans and jumpers that are a bit more expensive, although she makes out that they're her scruffy clothes. She's quite a looker, as well. Lots of dark hair hanging down – not permed or owt. She teaches night school and she goes on these anti-foxhunting marches, and some other marches as well. But she's too polite to keep you standing at her door for long.

"I've come to see Mick," I said. I suppose that was a bit unusual, because usually I ask if Mick is coming out, and I hang around on the doorstep until he does. But mostly he comes round for me.

"Oh," she says.

Then I got this fit of coughing, which was murder. I really wanted to cough, but if I let myself cough it was like being axed in the ribs and hit by a butcher's cleaver in my back.

She says, "Are you all right?" Which was a pretty daft question if you ask me, because I was clutching my ribs and trying not to explode and going, "Ah! Ah! Ah!" if I did cough (and that hurt almost as much as coughing!).

"You'd better come in then," she said, and dragged me into her living-room.

She got me some water.

For someone who wouldn't let Mick play with toy guns when he was little, she's got some pretty nasty pictures on her living-room walls. Well, they're posters really, of these kids half starved to death with their bellies swollen up like balloons, and of baby seals being clubbed to death with their brains all mashed in, and the worst is this photograph of this man shooting another man through the head, just at the moment he's shot him. Both the blokes look a bit Chinese. But it's the worst because the man who's doing the shooting, his eyes are quite black and clear. Not milky. He's doing it in plain cold blood. Not because he's lost his rag. I wouldn't have that picture up on my wall. Never in a month of Sundays.

Well, I stopped coughing at last, and I'm waiting for her to give Mick a shout – but she doesn't. She's all jittery, turning the radio on and off, and pretending to water the plants on the window-ledge, though you can see they don't need it because there's water in the saucers. And she keeps glancing at me out of the edge of her eye, like maybe I'm about to nick the silver and scarper.

So I said, "Is Mick in then?"

And she said, "He's doing his homework." Then she adds, sarcastic, "I suppose you've done all yours."

"I haven't got any to do," I said. "I've been off sick with pneumonia."

She went a bit red, and I could tell she was sorry she'd been sarky. But we weren't getting anywhere. Anyway, it sounded funny to me – Mick doing his homework on a Saturday.

So I said, "Can I go and say hello to him?"

And she swallowed quickly and said, "No. No. I'd rather you didn't. He's very busy."

"I'd best be off then," I said.

"I suppose you'd better," she said.

Then I said, just to be friendly, "It's good news about that letter, isn't it? I expect Mr Dalton's pleased and all."

That makes her look even more jittery. "It's too early to tell yet. Jim's gone back to Manchester to talk with the management."

"Great," I said. Then I went, feeling a bit odd. And I felt even odder when I looked up at Mick's bedroom window and caught a glimpse of him standing there, but he ducked down behind the curtains without even waving. And he's supposed to be my best mate!

I didn't feel like going home, so I caught the Number 27 into town and wandered round for about an hour, looking in shops such as Hamnet Lord and Sons, Gunsmiths and Fishing Tackle. They don't like you looking in there unless you buy something, so I bought some .22 waisted slugs for my air-rifle, and listened to this really posh grandfather buying this fishing-rod and all the gear for his grandson. He was a really nice old feller, proper class like gentry, but the lad was a nit who kept whining on that he'd sooner have a space invaders game because all the chaps at school had them. If I'd been the old feller I'd have wrapped the fishing-rod round the nit's neck and chucked him in the river.

I suppose my eyes must have been popping out on stalks at all the gear he was buying, because this old feller notices me, and he smiles like he's really really fed up, and I shrug and smile back, feeling sorry for him. He told Mr Hamnet just to wrap the lot up, and would he deliver it? Then he marches out of the shop with the nit trailing along behind, still whining on about space invaders.

I was just about to leave the shop as well, when Mr. Hamnet hands me two more tins of slugs – not the cheap ones, but Beeman Silver Jets, and says they're a present from the gentleman! Perhaps he thought I was someone else, but it was nice of him all the same.

Anyway, I was beginning to feel ropey, so I set off up Mill Street to catch the bus home. I waited at the bus stop which is just opposite the gates of Stone Cross, and there were two blokes waiting as well. The occupation was over at the mill, because everyone had gone home to think about the future like the new letter said, and you could see these great big white lorries with MAINTENANCE written on them, inside the locked gates.

These two blokes I'm waiting with at the bus stop are talking about it, saying it looks like they're doing a lot of work to the machinery at the mill, or maybe they think they've scared the living daylights out of the work force and it's all a con so that they can install robots without the unions making a fuss, because everyone will be so pleased to have a job who keeps one, even if it means cutting the work force by half. And it's all a bad do for Haverston either way. And they're suspicious as hell about what's going on, but what can they do about it? At least, says one, they've got all the big union men in Manchester, talking about it.

I just listened to this without taking much of it in, then the bus came and I went home, with three tins of slugs in my pocket for the price of one. But I remembered what those blokes said afterwards.

When I got home, Chunder was in. He'd come back from Kirkby Haverston with this scruffy looking little hen in a cardboard box tied up with string. It didn't look much to me, but he was that tickled about it, you'd have thought he'd given birth to it hisself! He kept saying, "Champion layer, this bird," and winking at me, like it was a great joke and a secret, which I suppose it was.

He wanted me to go up to the allotment with him, to help him build a special run and hen house for it before it got dark. To tell truth, I was feeling bloody rough by then, and I had to breathe very shallow and careful or it felt like someone was trying to saw me in half with a blunt hacksaw blade. But it was that good to see him in such fine fettle, and not even drunk, after the last few weeks, that I went up and gave him a hand.

I wasn't much use, but he was too pleased to notice. And we cobbled together this run inside the other run, and he made a box out of an old packing-case, with some tar cloth nailed round it, that would do for the time being. Then we filled it with newspaper and straw to make this scraggy hen cosy, and we sat in the shed for a while, so I could catch my breath, and so he could smoke a few fags.

"Eh, she's a beauty . . . Goose that'll lay the golden egg, that 'un, our Billy. Mother of champions . . ." he kept murmuring.

I felt like saying that I thought he'd been had. She didn't look as if she could fight her way out of a paper bag, didn't that bird, but I never said owt because, apart from anything else, Chunder does know what he's talking about when it comes to things like that.

He said he was going to leave it for a few weeks before he bought the stud cock, so as he didn't arouse any suspicions.

By then the stars were coming out. It was freezing. You could see your breath smoking in the cold air. I went on back, but Chunder had to stay up on the allotment, he was fretting that much about his hen catching a chill. He'd even given it a name, Alice, after my grandma who died before I was born, of a bad chest, and who Dad and Chunder say was an angel, and everyone else says she was an angel to put up with them the way she did.

Dad came home later, with a real mood on him. I thought maybe that Smith's sister wasn't as friendly towards him as he was towards her. And it didn't help when I asked him if he'd got some free tickets for the circus.

"Don't be blooming daft," he said. "Every circus in the country is in winter quarters this time o' year – apart from that mickey-mouse outfit. I've seen pantomime horses look more likely than the nags they've got there! I'll tell you what, Bill – RSPCA'll put a stop to that outfit when they get wind o' it! It's crooks like that give a bad name to circuses and fairs. I bet they haven't even got ruddy licences for their big cats!"

"I'm surprised Dancer Smith's travelling with them, then," I said.

"So am I, lad. So am I. But it sounds like the boss has got something on him that he's having to pay off. I'll tell you what, Bill, I'd give him the cash to pay his way out if I had any put by. Now what's fer tea?"

Well, the circus didn't perform at all in town. And that night, when I was almost asleep in my bed, I heard some stranger talking downstairs, who I guessed was Dancer Smith. He said the police had been sniffing round, and it serves that hedge-crawler of a boss right if he ended up in jail, and he wasn't going back to travel with them even if they did break every bone in his body.

Dancer wasn't there when I got up next morning, although it was obvious that someone had slept on the floor, because there was a pile of blankets, and Chunder was still asleep on the sofa.

But my Dad looked happier, and there was a letter tucked away behind the clock, which said:

'Hard you ben asking, Ned. I mite see yous in the sumer if we get up that way but don say anthin to anone yet,

luv,

Sal.'

It had vanished by dinner-time, so Dad hadn't meant anyone to see it, and I never said owt. But it gave me a funny feeling reading it. She sounded OK and I'm quite looking forward to seeing what she's really like if she turns up. But it made me feel strange all the same. I mean, I reckon they must be quite serious if they're writing letters and that.

I suppose it's just that I've got that used to it being Dad and me and Chunder, and no women, that sometimes I forget that Dad's nowhere near past it. I've even seen Mick Dalton's mam looking at him sometimes, and it makes you realise that Jim Dalton isn't a patch on my Dad to look at – especially when he's dressed up to go out of a Saturday night. He looks a bit Spanish in a suit. The funny thing is, I've only ever seen Mrs Dalton give him *that* sort of look when he's scruffed up, coming home from work in his jeans, with a six o'clock shadow on his chin. But she doesn't look like she fancies him so much when he's shaved and smelling of Brut, and in his Saturday suit. But then you can't tell with Mick Dalton's mam, because she's not really like other women round here.

It turns out that Mick has a black eye. It's a real shiner, a beaut. I saw him from the back, kicking an old tin can up the street, so I shouted, "Eh up, Micky!"

And he turned round, with a look on his face like he's daring me, just daring me, to say something about his black eye.

So I said, joking, "Your old lady been knocking you about or something!"

The next thing I know, I'm flat on the pavement, and Mick's kicking me in the ribs, yelling, "Mind your own business, can't you! Mind your own bloody business!"

I didn't even try and fight back. I curled up in a ball and tried to cover my ribs with my hands and elbows, and I thought I might die if he got the boot in my chest again.

Then, suddenly, I see Mick Dalton's feet fly up in the air, as if he'd been launched like a Saturn 5 rocket, then they come down again and dangle about a foot off the pavement.

It's my dad, and he's holding Mick by the back of his jacket.

Mrs Dalton comes bursting out of her own front door. "Leave him alone, you! Put him down or I'll fetch the police!" And she's calling Dad every name you can think of, and some you can't.

Dad put Mick down. He ignored Mrs Dalton, which was pretty good of him really when you take into account the things she was calling him. I got to my feet.

"I thought you and Mick were best mates," said Dad.

"We are," I coughed.

"Shut up, Mam!" said Mick Dalton. "Everyone's looking at you!" And his mam put her hand over her mouth and began to cry.

"I started it, anyhow," said Mick. "Didn't I, Bill?"

"I'm not right sure," I said, trying to straighten myself up and stop coughing. "What did you do that fer, anyhow?"

And Mick's mam started saying, "I'm so sorry, Mr Coward. I'm so sorry! I thought . . . I don't know – I thought you were – I'm so sorry . . . " and she rushed back into her house.

Dad shrugged and looked a bit baffled. I think we all looked a bit baffled, even Mick. But Dad catches hold of Mick by the jacket again, and drags him close up, and he hisses, "If I ever see you kicking my lad, or any poor bugger else when they're down, I'll give yer a clogging that'll take more than one lifetime to forget! Got it?"

"Yes, Mr. Coward," says Mick, looking a bit white.

"Good," says Dad. Then he walks off, because he doesn't want to interfere between mates, and he probably wouldn't have interfered at all except he knew I'd just had pneumonia.

"Sorry," says Mick. "She's been getting on at me. Everyone's been getting on at me. I just lost my rag."

"S'alright," I said. "How did you get that shiner anyway?"

Mick muttered, "Fell off me bike," and he gave the tin can a really vicious kick that made it fly right across the street and clang against the wall of Number 31 with a noise that made me wince, thinking of how that kick would have felt if it had still been me and not the can.

Well, it's obvious that he's lying about the black eye, but as I don't fancy being used as a human football again, I don't say anything, even though I'm a bit surprised. I mean, if he'd got it in a fight, he would have said, and if he'd really got it in an accident he wouldn't have been bothered about it. Which only left his mam and dad, and the funny way his mam had been behaving – jittery and nervous and all strung on edge. Which seemed to me to mean that his dad had given it to him.

I was quite shocked – a lot shocked, in fact. His mam and dad aren't like that. They don't have rows – leastways, not ones you can hear in the street. And they don't believe in corporal punishment. (I know that for a fact, because Jim Dalton threatened to take Mick away from school last term if the Head used the cane on him.) So it was a shock, in a way that it wouldn't have been a shock if Bob Eccles's old man had given him a black eye, or even if my old man had given me a black eye – which he never would do. Touch wood.

I felt right sorry for Mick, so I said come round my house and have some chips, Dad's just gone to fetch some from Danny's (who stays open Sunday dinner and does Roast Beef and Chips Specials £1.10.).

Mick's really nervous that my dad might hate him, which is daft. I told him it was daft – Dad didn't hate him, and would have forgotten all about it by now anyway.

I was right. We were all sitting there eating roast beef, chips, peas and gravy with an extra portion of chips (Mick was eating Chunder's, because Chunder had gone up to the allotment, and Dad said Chunder's belly wouldn't miss what his eyes hadn't seen). And we were having a can of Coke, and watching a film on the box about these prisoners-of-war in Japan blowing up a bridge, when Chunder comes staggering in.

"It's killed Alice!" he whispers, and he holds out this mess of blood and feathers for us to see.

We stopped eating. We just froze and stared, and the roast beef I'd been chewing I had to spit back into the carton, or I'd have been sick, I think.

Chunder looks as though he's going to have a heart attack. My dad took the dead hen from Chunder, wrapped it up in a piece of newspaper, along with his chips, and went and put it in the dustbin. Then he took Chunder to the sink and washed his hands for him, with lots of Fairy Liquid. The water in the sink went red. Then he led Chunder back to his chair, and poured some whisky into a mug, and made him drink it.

Mick and I were just staring at him. I was scared stiff that Chunder was going to have a stroke or a heart attack, because Dad was being so gentle with him. Dad must have thought the same.

"It's killt all me hens, Ned," Chunder whispers. "Every last one of them. It's killt 'em and tore 'em up, Ned!"

"What has?" says Dad, crouching down by Chunder's chair. "What's killed them?"

"How the hell do I know!" yells Chunder, then he covers his face with his hands, and his shoulders are going up and down, and I see a tear, or a bit of spittle, drop onto his knee.

You wouldn't think an old bloke like our Chunder could get that upset about a few scrawny hens. Chunder had had hens killed before, by local cats, and occasionally by foxes come down off the moor. He hadn't cried then – just got mad and built the fence round the hens even higher. But maybe this was worse because of that one new scratty bird that he had called after Grandma, or maybe it was because all the hens had been killed, or maybe it was just too much on top of all that about Stone Cross.

Anyway, Dad, Mick and me marched up to the allotment to see for ourselves, and what we saw wouldn't have made you cry. It would have made you feel a bit sick. It was like something out of one of those video nasties.

Chunder's posh hen house had been knocked over onto its side, and there were dead birds scattered all over the frozen mud, and some had jammed themselves into the wire-netting as if they were trying to escape. And the hens weren't just dead, they were ripped up. And some were scattered over the fence on the moor. Feathers were blowing across the allotments like brown snow. It was cold enough to snow, but there wasn't a cloud in the sky.

"Bloody hell . . ." murmured Dad, at last.

It looked like a whole pack of foxes had been let loose and gone into a frenzy, like sharks do when they smell blood. "Bloo-dy hell . . ." said Dad again.

That was the end of the C.E.C. Reclamation Scheme. Chunder wouldn't go up to the allotment any more, and can you blame him?

There was nothing we could do, apart from scrape up the hens off the frozen mud and put them in two old sacks. We couldn't even bury them because the ground was hard as concrete. It was horrible to begin with, but after shovelling up the first few hens, you sort of got used to it. They didn't smell much because of the cold – only the blood smelled a bit like wet rusty metal.

Mick suggested that Dad should get the police. But Dad said no, they wouldn't be interested in that sort of thing. (And, besides, Chunder wasn't really supposed to keep hens or any livestock on the allotments, although everyone knew he did and never said owt.)

Afterwards, Dad carried the sacks all the way to the river and slung them in because, like he said, we couldn't have buried them, and it would have scared the dustbinmen to death if we'd put them in our bin.

He had a grim look on his face, did Dad. I suppose we all had. Dad said he thought it must have been mink or polecats, and I said, but how did they get in, and Dad said they needed only the tiniest little hole and they'd get in.

Mick said, "But a polecat couldn't knock over the hen house, Mr Coward."

I went very cold when he said that.

But Dad reckoned maybe the hens themselves had knocked it over in their fright, trying to get out, which just seemed possible.

Dad went down to see how Chunder was getting on. Mick and me followed shortly after, because it was beginning to go dark, and it was pretty scary up there with the blood stains all over the hard mud.

We couldn't work it out. Chunder's hen run was built like Colditz. It had an eight foot chicken-wire fence all round, with barbed-wire on top of that. You had to get in through a red door with Number 102 on it, painted in yellow. And that door was padlocked. And the chicken-wire goes under the soil for about a yard to stop foxes and ferrets and tramps digging their way in.

Well, Mick and me had a good look round to see if we could see a hole, but we couldn't. And we were just about to go, when I noticed, high up on the barbed-wire, this little tuft of black fur. I hadn't noticed at first because there was that much down and feathers blowing about and stuck in the fence that you wouldn't notice, would you? But it was definitely fur, a tweak of it, like a bird might carry in its beak, up on the barbed-wire, on the moor side of the fence.

I showed Mick.

"Something must have climbed over," he said.

We set off at a run for home, because we were both thinking the same thing. Something must have climbed over – or jumped! And neither of us much fancied meeting a beast that could jump eight feet, especially in the dark.

What had happened on the allotment almost got into the *Haverston Gazette*, but not quite. Nobody actually rang up the newspaper and told them about it, but news travels fast in Haverston, and on Wednesday, just after I got in from school, there was a knock on the door.

Chunder answered it, and it was this lad called Chris Fairfield who had been in the same sixth form as Fats Grundy, and who was now working as a junior reporter for the *Gazette*.

"Good afternoon, Mr Coward," said Chris, very polite. "I heard that some sort of animal had killed your hens. I wondered if you would like to tell me about it? I'm from the *Haverston Gazette*."

"Oh?" said Chunder. Then he said in his best voice, "I'm sorry, but it's a very private grief." And closed the door on him. Then he said, "Sodding newspapers – always poking their noses into other folk's business!" So you can see, Chunder was feeling a lot better.

Not that it would have done Chris Fairfield much good even if he had got a story, because by Friday the newspaper was full of Stone Cross again.

The only other person to show some interest in Chunder's hens was the Haverston Valley River Warden. He's called Mr Wave, which always makes me laugh, because of him being to do with the river. Although I suppose it could be Wave, as in waving your hand. Anyhow, he came up because he was interested in the mink theory, and he was worried that if there were mink around, they might start killing ducks and trout etc. in the Spring. Mick and me took him up to the allotments, to save Chunder having to go, but there wasn't much to see. We'd even righted the hen house, so that the place didn't look so much like a disaster.

There were a few seagulls and a couple of rooks tidying up the odds and ends of hens that we'd left, but apart from that there wasn't anything to see. Even that tuft of fur had gone – either it had blown away, or some seagull had had a peck at it. And we didn't tell Mr Wave about it either, in case he thought we were making it up.

The ground was still frozen solid, and there were no footprints. There hadn't been any on the day the hens were killed, because Mick and me had looked.

Anyway, Mr Wave and Chunder had a cup of tea and a nice long chat about modern poachers who use cyanide in the water, and both of them thought that was a terrible thing to do, and not like the olden days when a poacher was a skilled craftsman.

And it was because of them sitting there nattering, and me listening, (thinking I might pick up some useful tips on catching trout, for when I come to do my Plan) that we missed watching the six o'clock news . . .

# Chapter 4

There comes this rumour in the shape of Danny from the chip shop, at about eight o'clock, after Mr Wave had gone.

"What's up, Dan?" said Dad, because Danny was standing at the front door with his sleeves rolled up and his apron on and his face all red and sweaty from leaning over the fryers, even though it's a freezing cold night. I could tell that my dad was thinking perhaps Danny had been vandalised, or had had his till money nicked by yobs.

"What's this about them taking all the machines out of Stone Cross, Ned?" said Danny.

"What?" said Dad.

"Charlie Eccles was saying something about it in the shop. Said he'd seen it on the news. Is he making it up, or what? I mean, you know what Charlie's like," said Danny.

"I dunno," said Dad, staring at Danny.

"Well, I just thought I'd pop out and ask while the shop was quiet, like. I thought maybe you'd know something – seeing as you work there and Charlie doesn't."

"What's that?" said Chunder, coming in from the kitchen.

"Danny says that Charlie Eccles says that they've taken allt' machinery out of Stone Cross!" said Dad, explaining.

"Well? Is it truth? Or what?" says Chunder, staring at Dad, who's staring at Danny, who's shrugging his shoulders. Me – I'm just listening, thinking that's just the sort of daft thing Charlie Eccles would say.

Then this rumour goes off down Long Moor Lane in the shape of Dad, Chunder, Danny and me. (Danny had left his Mrs and his daughter in the chip shop. He hadn't left it empty.)

And they're saying things like, "They wouldn't have done that. They couldn't have done that." And I'm thinking that it must be the first time in that joker Charlie Eccles's life that he's been taken seriously, and that it would end up a wild goose chase like the time Charlie Eccles told everyone they were giving free pints away at the *New Horseshoe Inn*, on account of the fact that the landlord's daughter was getting married. And it turned out she wasn't, and they weren't, and half of West Haverston was after Charlie's blood for a week, because it's a seven mile ride out to the *New Horseshoe*.

Dad goes and knocks at Number 23, the Daltons, and there's Chunder and Danny and me standing behind his shoulders like a bunch of heavies.

"Evening, Mrs Dalton," says Dad.

"Hello," says she, peeping round the door. She's just washed her hair and it smells lovely even from where I'm standing, though it makes her look a bit witchy in the face because it's wet and black.

"Hiya, Bill," says Mick, squinting under her elbow.

"What's this about them taking all the machinery out of Stone Cross, Mrs Dalton? Is Jimmy back?"

"What? No! No, he rang earlier to say that the management keep putting the delegation off. Something do to with some London firm of accountants not having arrived in time. They've postponed the meeting until Friday."

"Oh, and I expect the union'll pay his expenses to stay in a hotel," says Dad, in this really quiet, polite voice, that makes Mick stare at me, and me stare at the black curls on the back of my dad's head which are a bit orange with the street light on them.

"Hold on, Ned," says our Chunder.

And Mrs Dalton says, "Well . . . I don't know. I suppose they might."

"Did you hear what I said?" says Dad.

And Chunder says, "I said hold on, Ned! There's no use blaming the oily-rag for what the engineers have done!"

Mrs Dalton gives Chunder a look like he's something that's crawled up the plug hole, because she can't see that he's saving her from a very sharp edge of my old feller's tongue.

"Night, Mrs Dalton, lass," says Chunder, "sorry to disturb you."

It's not like my dad to start losing his rag with a woman like that, and for a moment I think it's because Mick's mam isn't like the other women round here, and then I realise that it's because he's scared that the rumour might be true, and he wants somebody to yell at him that it isn't true.

By then Mrs Dalton had closed her front door on us, but then Mick comes sneaking out.

And, would you believe it? It started to snow. They reckon it starts snowing when the weather begins to warm up, but it felt even colder if anything.

"Well, what next?" said Danny, rubbing his arms to keep warm.

"Reckon I'll go down *The Weaver's Arms*. See if there's any news," said Dad, who had cooled off a bit by then.

"I'd best get back to the shop," said Danny. "The Mrs isn't too good. She's had the 'flu."

"Aye. Night, Danny."

"Ned?" says Danny.

"What?"

"Oh," says Danny, flapping his arms, "you know what Charlie Eccles is like . . . "

Dad nodded. Then there's just Chunder and Dad and Mick and me, standing in the snow, looking down at the yellow glow of Haverston, and you can smell the exhaust fumes of the bus that's just gone from the stop.

Chunder says, "Listen, Ned. It's nothing that won't keep till morning. If it's true, it's true, and there's nowt we can do about it. And if it isn't then Charlie Eccles'll be laughing out o' wrong side o' his gob."

"If it isn't true," says Dad, "then it won't be his gob he'll be laughing out of!"

Chunder says, quietly, "I reckon I've had enough, Ned lad."

"I reckon you have, Dad," says my old feller. "Get home."

"What will you do, Dad, if it is true?" I said.

"Dunno," says Dad. "I'll cross that bridge when I get to it, and it'll be every man for hisself."

Then my dad goes walking off into the snow and the shadows and the patches of light under the street lamps, until he's only a head and shoulders going down hill, then he's only the top of a head, and then he's gone.

Mick says to Chunder, "My mam doesn't know anything."

"I know, lad. I know," says Chunder.

"Night, Bill," said Mick, and let himself back in his front door.

"Night, Mick," I said. Then I went home with Chunder to wait.

It was true. And nobody was laughing about it in West Haverston, not even Charlie Eccles. Those vans that had MAINTENANCE on them were nothing of the kind. They were men dismantling machines and taking out components so that the machines they couldn't move wouldn't work any more, and shifting stock out of the stock room, and taking patterns out of the cutting rooms, and all the papers out of the gaffer's offices. And Stone Cross was left as empty as a busker's hat with only a few coppers rattling around in it, and the canteen chairs.

And there was nobody to kill and nobody to blame, because the people who wanted killing and blaming didn't live in Haverston. Jim Dalton had been right, and everybody knew it wasn't his fault. I mean, once the thing had really happened, people began to feel guilty that they hadn't listened to what he'd been saying for the last three or four years. But that didn't stop Mick's dad from blaming himself and ending up the way he has.

The thing that had happened was so big and sneaky that even my old feller didn't get drunk or lose his rag. He just came home, with snow all on his shoulders, and said, "It's true. It really is true. Can you believe that?" And he went to bed.

Nobody on our street expected it, I don't think, because even Jim Dalton hadn't heard of anything like that happening before. And you can't expect what's never happened. You can't even say it was like something that happened when . . . Or, that reminds me of . . . Unless you're as old as Chunder. And he said, "That's what happened when they closed the foundry when my father were a lad, and they said they couldn't believe it then."

Another letter came, and you knew what it would say even before you opened it. It said something like, "Ha-ha! You weren't expecting that, were you? Now try occupying Stone Cross and see where that gets you! And if you're very good we might settle up with you, when it suits us, and, meantime, you'll have to live on credit. Have a nice day!"

So Dad didn't bother to open it and chucked it on the fire.

The whole of Long Moor Lane was silent as a Christmas card under the snow, and everyone was regretting what they had spent at Christmas because there wasn't that kind of cash to hand now, or ever again as they could see.

Chunder was badly, so he had my bed, and I went to sleep on the sofa for a few nights. Then, one night, I found myself half way upstairs, with Dad trying to carry me, and I slept in his bed with him. It was a bit of a squash but it was better than sleeping in the dark downstairs. And Dad said I kicked him like a mule all night. I said he snored like a pig. And he said he'd sleep on the sofa if it would make me more comfy, but I said no.

And, at school, Oggy said, "What's the matter with you, Coward? My scintillating discourse putting you to sleep?"

"Sorry, Sir. Just thinking," I said, and tried to keep awake.

After class, he said, "How's the chest?"

"It still hurts a bit, but it's OK"

"And how's your grandfather these days?"

"Not so bad. But he's fretting about his hens."

As I was about to go, he said, "Oh, Coward. Try and make sure you give me a sick note if you're off."

"Why, Sir?" I thought that would make him laugh, but it didn't.

"You've heard of social workers?"

"I'll bring you a sick note," I said.

"Good lad. Oh, and Coward, what about that homework?"

"Homework?" I said.

"What the hell," said Oggy, and stared at the ink stains on his desk.


Then it comes March 3rd. My birthday, that is. Dad said (and he was screwing up this leaflet from the dole office that had come uninvited through the door), "What do you want for your birthday, lad?"

That set me thinking, just for one minute, and I thought of all the fishing tackle that old geezer had bought in Hamnet Lord and Sons, and how it might turn out I was a long lost relation of his, and of this knife I'd seen in their window with about fourteen gadgets, and of this bomber jacket I'd seen, and of . . . Oh, I don't know what. Because I was trying not to think about what I really wanted.

And Dad asked again. He asked fierce. "Come on! Out with it! What do you want?"

"Leave him alone," said Chunder, who was wrapped in blankets watching the box.

And there's a look on my dad's face that I've never seen before

– like he's trying to hurt himself. Or make me say something that'll hurt him.

"Come on! You must want something!"

And I felt like I was seeing him through blue silky smoke – not him really, but the thing that was trying to make him hurt himself.

So I said, "I want a shot gun, like in the window of Hamnet Lord and Sons. Or I want a racing bike! Mark Johnson's dad bought him a video for his birthday – but you'd never buy me anything like that!"

"That's what I thought," said Dad, and dropped down on the sofa.

Then the smoke clears, and I can see that it's not me that's winning, and it's not Dad that's winning, it's the thing that's trying to make him hurt himself that's winning.

I said, "I'm only joking, Dad. I don't want any of them things."

"What do you really want?" said Chunder.

"I want a lurcher pup," I said, not meaning to. "I want one that I can train myself."

Dad sighs, looking at me, then looking at the floor and putting his hands either side of his face. "You can't get a good lurcher for less than fifty quid . . ."

I knew that. So I said, in a hurry, "But I don't want it until I've left school because I wouldn't have the time to train it when I was at school. And I wouldn't have the time to use it, neither."

Dad said, quiet as whispering, "What can I give you then, Billy?"

I said, "I dunno, Dad. It doesn't matter."

"Tell you what," said Chunder. "What if we give you some cash, and you can stash it under your mattress, to save up, like, for this dog you want?"

"Great!" I said, but it didn't feel great, because I'd told them what I really wanted when I hadn't meant to say anything at all.

"Aye! Here's a fiver," said Dad, smiling.

"And take another out of me jacket," says Chunder. So I did, and I had two blue ones, crisp as Izal, and I stashed them under the stair carpet, because I didn't really have a mattress to stash them under, seeing as Chunder was sleeping in my bed, and I was sleeping in Dad's.

That was the first night I dreamed about the Beast. It was trying to bite the back of my head. It was a terrible, frightening prickly feeling, and I daren't look round. But it was probably only my dad's chin pressing against my neck.

Then, a couple of days later, the Beast killed Mr Eccles's dog, and some cats. Mick told me about it. I didn't really believe it, but it gave me and Mick something to talk about that hadn't anything to do with Stone Cross or our dads.

Mick said he'd seen these claw prints in the snow, and I pretended to believe him. We even went out a little way onto the moor, so he could show me, but he couldn't find them again, and he said it was on account of the fact that it had snowed in the night. It was weird being on the moor in winter all the same, and we came back quickly.

Mick said, "You don't believe me."

"Yes I do."

And he says, "They didn't believe me dad neither!"

I said nothing, because I didn't think it was fair bringing that up then, and what could you say after all? His dad had been right.

It was funny sort of weather for March. It snowed and snowed, until it was so thick and deep that buses and cars couldn't get up the hill to Long Moor Lane.

People started popping round to each other's houses to borrow things, and then they'd stay for a chat, until, in the end, you'd get a couple of families sitting round someone's kitchen talking about this and that (mostly about Stone Cross and the dole), and taking it in turns to yell at the little kids. Chunder said it was getting like the olden days again. We even had a week off school because the boiler broke down. All the news on telly was about the late snow bringing the country to a halt – a Welsh farmer hanged himself because he couldn't bear to dig any more lambs out of the drifts. And this couple, snogging in the back of a car, got frozen to death (somewhere down South), only it turns out that the woman is the wife of the vicar and it's a real scandal . . .

There were rallies and marches and meetings in the town centre about Stone Cross, but it was hard for the folks on Long Moor Lane to get to them, although Jim Dalton, who was back from Manchester, was always in the thick of them. He'd made this camp-bed up at the Trades Hall.

And Mick just went on and on and on about the Beast, until I got fed up of hearing about it. He even pretended he'd seen it from his bedroom window. He said it was gigantic with yellow eyes. Then the next day he said it had green eyes. I almost forgot about Chunder's hens, because the Beast he was talking about wasn't the Beast that had done that. It was like his own customised Beast he'd made up for himself – just like a little kid playing at Scary Monsters!

Then there was a bit of a thaw for a few days. These blokes came over from Kirkby Haverston in a battered old land-rover, to see Chunder. They were a rough looking lot of old lads, I can tell you, but Chunder was pleased as punch to see them. They'd brought him a new hen to make up for Alice, because they had heard what had happened to the hens, and to Stone Cross.

At first Chunder wouldn't take it, but they said the first hen he'd bought had had some kind of a disease and would have died anyway. So they'd bought this new bird as a replacement because they didn't want the Cock Fighting Fraternity to get a reputation for swindling people. Of course, they were making it up about the disease and that, just to make it easier for Chunder to accept the bird without it seeming like charity.

Chunder sent me round to the off-licence to get a couple of

cans and a bottle of whisky. What he paid for in drinks would have more than paid for the hen – but that wasn't the point.

Well, it got a bit like Christmas in our house that evening, with these old fellers drinking and singing and playing cards and spitting into the fire for luck-of-the-devil. You could tell they were mostly farm workers and shepherds because they had hands like bunches of brown sausages, like farmers get from working out in all weathers.

They got talking about what had killed Chunder's hens, and it turns out that something had been worrying the sheep up Kirkby Haverston way and over Hardale, which is just a few miles further on. (It's very wild bleak country, is Hardale. You don't get many people going up that valley, even in Summer.)

Anyway, something had killed a couple of pregnant ewes, and another flock of sheep had been that scared by something and chased about that one or two of them had dropped their lambs.

They reckoned it was a dog, or a couple of dogs. In fact, one farmer had shot an Alsatian which he'd seen running across the fell side. This turns out to be Charlie Eccles's old Alsatian that he'd been taking for a walk. (So much for Mick's Beast having killed it!) And, although Charlie was very upset, as you can imagine, the farmer wouldn't give him any compensation. He said it was his own fault for letting the dog off the lead when there's sheep around, especially as it's coming on lambing season.

I listened to all this – to these old lads arguing forwards and backwards about foxes and dogs and the law, with the firelight shining in their eyes and filling their wrinkles with black shadows.

The next day I told Mick about Charlie's dog having been shot. He said but what about them cats, then?

And then I had this very queer thought. I was looking at him. He had been acting a bit funny ever since his old man got back from Manchester, and he had had that strange grin on his mouth whenever he talked about the Beast.

"I reckon," I said, slowly, "that someone must have killed those cats."

"What do you mean?" says Mick, getting all jumpy and looking as if he might try to use me as a human football again. "What yer getting at?"

"Ah, nowt," I said and shrugged. But the thought that had come to me was that Mick had killed those cats. It was hard to believe, but that's what I thought. And I still reckon I was right, although he never admitted it. No more cats got killed though, except the usual one or two who got run over. It made me feel strangely about Mick for quite a long time, even though he stopped going on about his Beast so much, and even though he came to live with us for a time shortly afterwards.

# *Chapter 5*

After that thaw it started up snowing again. Sometimes Mick was at school and sometimes he wasn't, and even when he was I didn't spend so much time with him, because of what I had been thinking about those cats. Besides, Mick wasn't being too friendly – he said he didn't want me going round his house calling on him any more. I thought his mam had probably been getting at him but, as I say, I wasn't that bothered about seeing him just then.

Dad came in one evening, feeling fed up. He'd been all the way over to East Haverston in the snow to see this feller who owned a garage and who had once said to my dad that if he ever wanted a job to go and see him. It turns out that when Dad does want a job this feller says times are hard for everyone just now and he can't take him on. It's a long way over to East Haverston, and it was snowing like the North Pole, so you can see why he was fed up.

He cheered up soon enough, saying it wasn't the end of the world, and he never really fancied working in a lousy garage anyway. I made this huge pan of sausages that one of Chunder's Kirkby Haverston friends had dropped in on his way back from market. (Great sausages they were and all – not your pink plastic ones.) And we'd all settled down to eat our way through a mountain of sausage sandwiches and watch the telly, when there came this banging on our front door. Not just knocking – but banging.

Dad went to the door with a sausage butty in his hand, and he was having to lick the edges to stop the hot butter and tomato sauce running out.

It was Mrs Dalton, Mick's mam, and she was in a right state. "Mr Coward! Mr Coward! I can't get Jim to come in! Oh God! He'll freeze to death!"

"Here. You'd best come inside," said Dad.

"No! I can't!" cried Mrs Dalton. "Oh God! I don't know what to do! He's over at the bus stop . . . He'll freeze to death!"

Dad goes out onto the pavement and so do I. And there was Jim Dalton walking up and down in front of the bus stop in the dark and in the snow with nothing on but his underpants, and he was talking to himself, and sometimes shouting. You would think it would be a funny sight, but I'm telling you it wasn't. It was sort of scary and sort of sad. It made you feel sad for him.

"He won't listen to me," said Mrs Dalton. "Please Mr Coward, will you try and get him in – I'm scared he's going to hurt himself."

"Don't fret," said Dad. "I'll fetch him. Is he drunk, lass?"

Mrs Dalton shook her head. "No. I think he's having a nervous breakdown . . . " she said quietly, staring at her old man, who had started banging on the bus shelter with his hands. "Please, please, fetch him. But don't hurt him!"

"Eh, lass," said my dad, looking at her, "I sometimes think you've got wrong impression of me."

He took Chunder's coat off the peg in the hallway, and went over the road and leant on the bus shelter near poor Jim Dalton. He was still eating his sausage sandwich and he looked like he was pretending to wait for the bus. Mrs Dalton stayed by me, and I could see Mick standing at his front door, but he was too far away for me to see his face.

We could hear Dad speaking, just ordinary, to Jim Dalton, just as if he's waiting for the bus. "Eh up, Jimmy. I'll be glad when Spring comes round. You going down *The Weaver's Arms*?"

If you had closed your eyes, you wouldn't have known that Jim Dalton was standing there, damn near naked as a nail. Mick's dad just stares at my old feller, and his naked arms are dangling down by his poor thin ribs and his beer-belly.

Dad says, "Here, why don't you borrow me coat? You don't look right properly dressed for this weather, Jimmy. Go on, borrow it till we get to *The Weaver's*. I'll be all right in me jacket."

Jim Dalton took the coat and put it on, and his bare feet stuck out from under it.

"Tell you what, mate," says Dad, "how about coming round my place for a drink instead? I don't reckon the bus is going to get up the hill in this." Then, quite slowly, he put his arm round Jim Dalton's shoulders. He's a bit taller than Jim is my dad, but not a lot.

Then, suddenly, Jim Dalton turned his face and pressed it into Dad's jacket, and we could hear him making these strange croaking mewing noises. It's like hearing a seagull flying over the chimney pots – mewing and croaking like that. Dad brought Jim Dalton back to our house. Chunder gave him his seat by the fire and fetched some blankets. Mrs Dalton ran to her house and phoned for the doctor. And Mick just stood in the doorway staring at his dad, and tears kept dripping off his chin. I don't think it was soft him crying like that. I think maybe I would have cried if I'd seen my old feller in that state.

So the doctor came, and he took Jim to a special hospital for fellers who have nervous breakdowns.

Dad arranged with Mrs Dalton for Mick to stay with us for the time being, so that she could go to the hospital too, to keep an eye on what they were doing to Jim. "We'll have to fetch Mick's bed over though," Dad explained, but he didn't tell her it was because there were already three of us sharing two beds.

That was all arranged. Mick and I were back in my room (and I was in my own bed again) and Chunder was in Dad's bed, and Dad took his turn at sleeping on the sofa.

Mick was very quiet at first, and he lay awake at night with his eyes open. I could see them shining a bit in the dark. It was bad for him at school for a few days because word had got round that his dad had gone mental and had been carted off to the loony bin. But there weren't any fights. Mick didn't have enough spirit in him to fight – which was probably a good thing. If he'd risen to them they'd have kept on and on about it.

Chunder was the best with Mick. (I was awkward at thinking of things to say, although I forgave him a bit about the cats, because it was obvious things had been pretty weird in his house for quite a while, and maybe that's what made him take it out on the cats.) Chunder got Mick to help him make a hutch for this new hen. The hen had been living in a cardboard box in the kitchen up to then, because Chunder didn't want to risk putting her out in the snow.

The new hen was called Betty. I don't know of any Bettys so I expect it was one of Chunder's old flames she was named after. I was put out when he got Mick to help him and not me. Then I saw what he was up to – nattering on to Mick about this that and the other and the olden days, and getting Mick to do something instead of sitting on his bed all the time.

It was good for Chunder as well to have someone new to tell his stories to, because I knew most of them off by heart by then.

Mick began to cheer up. He didn't want to go and see his old man in hospital though, even though his mam came round and said he could if he wanted. Mrs Dalton could see he was better left where he was for the time being, so she didn't come round much, although she insisted on doing all of our washing in her washing machine and tumble drier (which saved me going down to the laundrette). And she gave Dad some money for Mick's food. Dad said she didn't have to. But she said she did.

One night, we were lying awake in the dark. Mick said, "It's a bit like being brothers, isn't it?"

"I suppose so," I said.

"Chunder says that in the olden days they used to wrap an eel skin round your arm if you sprained your wrist . . . I reckon we should remember things like that for when we go and live up on the moors."

"I suppose so," I said. I'd known that about eel skins ever since I was little.

"Chunder says he'll show us how to make a rabbit snare," murmured Mick.

"I'll show you if you like," I said.

He turned onto his side, making the bed springs creak. "Do you really know how to?"

"Yes."

"I wish we were brothers . . . " said Mick. "Don't you?"

That was a very awkward question to answer just then, so I pretended I hadn't heard and changed the subject. "You done that homework for Oggy?"

"What homework?" said Mick, and fell asleep.

Mick stopped talking about the Beast. He sort of forgot about it overnight, and life just went on for a while. Even the weather seemed to have got it in for Haverston – when the snow went, it stayed cold and windy and grey. On the telly they started showing things about the first signs of Spring – pictures of lambs when they read the weather forecast, and of daffodils and that. It wasn't like that up our street, I can tell you, but then the lambing season is always later up on the moors than it is everywhere else.

Stone Cross stopped being on the front page of the *Gazette*, and although there had been one or two strikes round town in sympathy, the blokes on strike didn't like to stay out too long, in case someone sneaked in and nicked their production lines as well. And you can't really blame them for thinking like that after what had happened.

Dad and Chunder did go down to the dole office in the end. First, they got their redundancy cheques. Chunder said it was blood money and spat on it, but he went and put it in the post office all the same – into what he calls his Weddings and Funerals Fund. Dad said it was more than he expected but not enough to keep us in the manner to which we were accustomed. He went out and bought a new bed. (There was a row about that. Dad reckoned Chunder should have bought a new bed seeing as he'd moved in with us, and not the other way round.) Then there was a row on and off for about a week about whether or not they should sign on – sometimes one calling it charity and sometimes the other. In a way Mrs Dalton made up their minds. She said it was their money that they had paid in National Insurance, and what did they think the unions and her old feller had been working their hearts out for for the last hundred years?

So they went, and they came back very quiet and thoughtful. And all Dad said to Chunder was, "I told you there'd be a queue."

But Chunder wouldn't say anything about it at all.

For some reason I began to get more and more on the wrong side of teachers at school. It got round that I was a bad influence on Mick. I suppose because he stopped handing in homework – but that wasn't fair. Just because he used to hand it in doesn't mean that he did it. Mostly, he'd copy off Peter Hargreaves, and when he did do it himself it was only because his mam and dad made him, and not because he was interested.

Anyway, there am I, being a bad influence on him at school and teaching him how to cook in the evenings, because he hardly knows how to fry an egg, let alone gut a fish cleanly. The trouble is, once some teachers get an idea like that into their heads they won't leave it alone. They just decide you're a bad influence or a trouble-maker, and it's hardly got anything to do with you at all. And even if you ask a question about something you're interested in they think you're trying to take the micky and tell you to stand outside, or something just as daft.

Of course, in the end, these teachers decide to put the boot in, and send a letter to my dad. (No prizes for guessing who wrote it. Twanger Harrison.) It says something like, Would he have a word with me for leading young Michael Dalton into trouble?

Dad said, "What's all this about?"

I tried to explain, but trying to explain something that daft to someone as sensible as my dad is like trying to explain that joke about "What's the difference between a duck?" to someone who doesn't think it's funny.

I got a clout – not a hard one, but a clout all the same. What do you think of that? Mick Dalton stops doing his homework, and I get clouted for it! Ah well, what the hell, as Oggy says.

All the same, I was pretty glad one way and another when Mick went back to live with his mam, and everything could get back to normal with Chunder, Dad and me.

Mind you, by then I wasn't thinking much about school and neither was Mick, because a new rumour had come into Long Moor Lane, in the shape of the Haverston Beast.

This is how it began (although I suppose it really began with Chunder's hens). Dad had bought a *Gazette* to look for a job in the employment column – it only took him about five minutes to read it, because there were only three jobs going and two of those were Saturday jobs for shop girls.

Dad happened to notice the name of a farmer that one of Chunder's Kirkby Haverston mates used to work for before he retired. And the headline was, DOUBLE TRAGEDY FOR LOCAL FARMER.

"Here. Listen to this," said Dad. "You know Harry Fletcher up Hardale way, who Bill Howgill used to work for?"

"Aye," said Chunder. "What about him?"

"Seems like he lost damn near half his ewes in that blizzard."

"That's a bad do," said Chunder.

"And that's not all," said Dad." Seems like he lost another two sheep to this here sheep-worrier. This dog. Says here he'd

73

never seen anything like it. It had eaten lamb right out of one ewe and broken the back of the other. It was still alive when Harry found it. Had to shoot that one, it says here."

"Must be a bloody big dog," says Chunder. "Here. Let me have a read."

"Wait on. Wait on," says Dad. "Let me just find out who won the darts match."

Well, that sets Chunder off about how in the war in the olden days, this dog with rabies had got in the trenches and bitten one of the soldiers and he'd died screaming blue bloody murder if anyone brought water near him. And the sad thing was that this soldier was due to go home on leave when it happened. And it's God's honest truth he's telling because his father had told him, and his father never told a lie in his life. I was glad Mick wasn't there to hear that story. He was back with his mam by then.

It caught my attention. Not at first, but when I was in the dark in bed. I heard in my head, "Must be a bloody big dog," and saw, like a picture, clear as a picture, that tuft of black fur caught on the barbed-wire that Mick and me had never told anyone about.

"Harry Fletcher's sheep!" said Bill Howgill, next time he popped in to visit Chunder. "That's just the thin end of the iceberg, that is!"

(Old Bill Howgill has the sort of voice that makes you think he must smoke about sixty fags a day, but, in fact, he's a Methodist and he doesn't smoke and he only drinks whisky for his arthritis in his hip, and he breeds fighting cocks for something to do in his old age.)

"Why, what's to do?" said Chunder.

"It's hard times," said Bill Howgill. "It's like there's a war going on up Kirkby Haverston and Hardale way. There's that much barbed-wire going up, and that many rumours flying round."

"What sort of rumours, Mr Howgill?" I said. "Do you want sugar in your tea?"

"No thanks. I'm sweet enough as it is. Now then, I'll tell you what rumours, young feller-me-lad. Well, you know Josh Lacey? He's lost two or three ewes and this old Swaledale ram that he was right proud of. Not that it was up to much these days, but it was a county prize winner in its time. Well, there's not many dogs that'll tackle a ram, is there? It was old, like I say, bit of a family pet really, but it wasn't that old . . . "

Chunder nodded and supped his tea. "Aye, you're right there, Bill. There's not many dogs'll take on a ram. Unless maybe there's a couple of them, working together . . . Something with a bit of collie in them, maybe?"

"Well," said Bill Howgill. "You know that queer old woman, that Buddhist, that took Crag Cottage? You know, that one whose husband was some sort of writer bloke? Aye, well, she come flying down into the village, saying that she'd seen the devil looking in her front window! Staring in through the lace curtains!"

"Baah!" said Chunder, disbelieving.

"That's what I said. I never knew these Buddhists believed in the devil, and if they don't then it's about time they did! That's what I say. But the funny thing is this – the same afternoon, Annie Jackson comes into the post office and starts telling Mrs Beck – you remember Mrs Beck, Charlie? She used to be a grand dancer in her time – where was I?"

"You were saying about Annie Jackson," I said.

"Oh aye. Well, she starts telling Mrs Beck that her youngest – Dawn, I think she's called – Dawn or Sarah, eh damn! I can't just remember which – had come screaming into the kitchen saying she'd seen a 'thingy' down by the beck. A 'thingy' drinking water out of the beck, and that she doesn't know what to do with the child, because she won't go out of the house, and she keeps screaming if her mam – that's Annie Jackson – even goes out into the garden. Well, Mrs Beck is a sensible body of a woman, and she says that it's just a phase and the little lass'll grow out of it."

"I expect she's right there and all," said Chunder. Then he winked at me. "Our Billy used to be scared of the loo flushing when he was a little lad. Used to pull chain and run for it, with his pants round his knees!"

I went a bit hot. They both laughed.

"Aye, well. But that's not the only thing," said Bill Howgill. "Can you wring another cup out o' that teapot? Grand. Ta. You know – well probably you don't know, because he's new round here – Paul Wakefield? He's working for the Major up at Hardale Hall. Working in the stables. He's a grand lad by all accounts. He came into *The Cocks* and said he was sure something had been sniffing round the stables in the night. He said he'd heard it, and that the Major's hunter had started kicking up a fuss, and it had taken him half the night to calm him down. Well, he doesn't strike me as the sort of lad that's given to lying. He said he'd actually heard something sniffing! He sleeps in tack room, does Paul. Got it very cosy he has too – it's like a little modern bungalow in there."

"Well, it all sounds a bit something and nothing to me, Bill," said Chunder. "Sheep being killed is one thing, a serious thing, but it's happened before and it'll happen again when you've got towns and sheep in spitting distance. But as for t'other, I'd not puddle me mind with it."

"Reckon you're right, Charlie," said Bill Howgill. "But when you've all been cut off for weeks on end by the snow, rumours start up and get round, and don't settle until Spring gets a good hold. Anyway, I best get back. You'll be coming over to *The Cocks* on Saturday?"

"Aye. Now the buses are running again."

"Good enough. I'll fix a lift back for you. Night, Charlie. Night, Billy, lad."

"Night, Mr Howgill."

"Oh," added Mr Howgill when he got to the door. "Did Ned have any luck with that garage job?"

Chunder just pulled a face. And the old lad shrugged, shook his head, and went off over the moors in his battered Morris Minor.

That was the second night I dreamed about the Beast. I heard it roaring softly, far away in the darkness, coming closer. But I expect it was just my dad snoring in the next room.

# Chapter 6

Next, the Beast got into the playground. I don't mean the actual creature itself, but the rumour of it. Some of the kids at school come by bus off the villages up the moors and other places round about, because they don't have schools up there any more like they used to in the olden days. I think maybe it was us kids who gave the thing its name. The Haverston Beast.

There's this lad in the next form, he's called Martin Clough, and he lives in a cottage in the valley on from Hardale. His folks are off-comers really, from Manchester, and his dad reads the news on Border telly. (He goes on and on about his dad, does Martin, like he was some great film star.) Anyway, it gets round that he's seen the Beast. He keeps dropping hints as big as buses until enough people are interested, then, one dinner time, we're all in the bike shed, ready to listen.

When it comes to the crunch, it turns out that he hasn't actually seen the Beast at all, but that he's seen a long line of tracks in the snow. He said he and his sister had gone down into Kirkby Haverston one night to see some friends, when they noticed these deep claw prints as big as your hand, coming out of the churchyard and going off up the fell towards Hardale Hall. It was snowing, he said, and him and his sister had followed the prints round the back of *The Hare and Hounds*, but they didn't fancy going any further in the dark.

"Ah, give over!" I said. "You never saw no Beast after all! You said you'd seen it!"

"I never," he said. "I said my sister *said* she *thought* she'd seen it. We were just going back round the front of the pub, and she said, 'What's that?' I turned to look, but she said, 'It's gone now. It was up there, on the fell – something black!'"

All the little kids are staring at him, like they're really scared.

"It were probably a sheep," I said. In my mind, though, I'm seeing a tuft of black fur on barbed-wire, dead hens . . . And hearing Chunder say, it must be a bloody big dog . . .

"Maybe," says Martin Clough, "maybe not. But we saw the footprints, didn't we?"

"I bet no one else saw them," I said.

"As a matter of fact, they didn't. The snow covered them up so quickly."

I shrugged my shoulders, and some of us were about to walk away (not the little kids though) when he says, "That's not all! I've heard it!"

"Oh aye," I says. "What was it doing – singing jingle bells?"

"No," said Martin. "It was one night. I woke up. Something had woken me up, and I heard it."

"Ger on!" I said.

"It went Oowwrooo-grrrr-oooowwr! A bit like a wolf, but not as howly – deeper it was, growling."

I'll give Martin Clough one thing – he's a pretty good storyteller, and when he made that noise it fair gave you goose-pimples on your arms.

I squatted down on my heels, trying to decide whether or not to believe him. "What were these tracks like, anyhow?" I said.

"Well, there's not much point trying to describe them to you," said Martin. "I mean, town people don't know about spoors and country things."

That got up my nose! "Come on," I said. "What size was the pad, about? How many claws did it have? How far apart? How long was its stride?"

"Oh," says Martin, pretending to think, "hard to say really. You see the thing was – I'd never seen anything like them before!"

It put a shiver down your spine, that did, even though you could tell he was making it up – at least, he was making some of it up.

"What's this, what's this?" says Oggy, poking his head round the side of the shed. "The Vandals Incorporated Annual General Meeting?"

All the little kids ran for it. They were that scared they'd have died if anyone had said boo to them.

"Come on you lot – out of there!" growled Oggy, sounding more like the Haverston Beast even than Martin. We wandered off.

Then other kids started saying they'd seen it – or heard it, or that their brother or their sister or their Aunty Maud had seen it. And one kid even said it had stolen their next-door-neighbour's baby out of its pram! (I know where that kid lives, and I know his next-door-neighbour, and if you ask me, it wasn't the Beast that did it, it was social workers.)

You know what it's like round the beginning of March on a wet day. It's almost dark some afternoons when you get out of school. Kids started walking home in gangs – even kids that hated each other but happened to live in the same street. You wouldn't believe it, but that's what they did, especially the little kids in the first year.

And kids started bringing knives to school in case the Beast attacked them on the way home. That caused a lot of trouble, because about a week later or so the Head got wind of what was going on, on account of the fact that Twanger Harrison had dragged this lad to his office. This kid had been carving his name in his desk with the point of a nine inch blade one lunch time. Although the knife was big, the lad wasn't, and the Head had him in tears in less time than it takes him to reach for his cane.

There were STERN WORDS in assembly. The Head doesn't want to hear any more of this nonsense, etc. That was on Thursday.

On Friday, the front page headline in the *Gazette* was HAVERSTON BEAST STRIKES AGAIN.

Dad said the headline made it sound as though there was a sex-maniac on the loose – which was probably why the *Gazette* wrote it like that, because people buy newspapers that have things about sex-maniacs in them. I mean, it's more interesting than the price lambs are fetching in market and how vandals ruined the parish church flower show, isn't it?

Dad had bought the paper for the employment column again (although I reckon he could have looked at that in the shop, seeing as there were only two jobs advertised – hairdresser's apprentice, and gardener/handyman one day a week must have own car).

Dad's got other things on his mind, and once he's realised that it isn't about a sex-maniac he doesn't bother to read any more of the paper. He just sits with his arms on the table, looking down at his hands. Then he starts writing L-O-V-E and H-A-T-E on his knuckles with my school felt-tip, then he goes into the kitchen and scrubs it off again, and goes back to sitting at the table, staring at his scrubbed raw hands.

I read the paper to Chunder while he worked out the score-draws for his coupon.

"Local farmers are expressing their growing concern about sheep-worrying in the area. Mr Joshua D. Lacey of High Dale Head Farm said, 'This has been the worst Spring since 1963–1964 for shepherds already. The snow came at just the wrong time for everyone, and now shepherds are having to protect their ewes from marauding dogs as well. I can't see where it will end. People could go bankrupt if this goes on.'

"More than a dozen sheep have been killed in the last few weeks, and many more animals have been found in an exhausted state. One Alsatian has already been shot, but farmers say this is only the tip of the iceberg.

"'Something must be done,' said Mr William Howgill, a retired shepherd. 'Folks can't sleep in their beds at night for worrying about what they will find in the morning.' And local housewife and mother of three, Mrs Anne Jackson said, 'If it's killing sheep then it can kill children. My children won't be safe until this killer is shot. I daren't let my toddlers out of my sight.'

"The police are looking into the matter, but they say their investigations are being hindered by a number of hoax calls, mostly from schoolchildren. They appeal to the public to be sensible and reassure them that there is no cause for alarm. 'It happens every year,' said Superintendent Cookson. And the local dog warden told the *Gazette* that since the recent large-scale redundancies in Haverston he has had to deal with more strays than ever. 'Some people can't afford to feed their dogs any more, and have started turning them out onto the streets rather than have them humanely put down.'

"We asked local farmers if they believed the work to be that of one dog or of a pack.

"'It's hard to say,' said Harold Fletcher, who has lost four sheep to the killer.

"'I wouldn't like to say at this moment.' And he warned dog-owners to keep their pets on the lead. 'We're shooting to kill,' he said. 'It's within our rights, and people's livelihoods are at stake.'"

"It's just like old Bill said," says Chunder. "Eh, our Billy," he added, "they're making a real scholar of you at that school. It's a right nice reading voice you've got." He smiled at the back of my dad's head, but Dad didn't turn round. "What's to do, Ned?"

"Nowt," said Dad.

"Good enough," said Chunder, and started putting ticks on his coupon.

"It seems to me they've got bloody short memories round here!" said Dad. "Seven hundred folks lose their jobs, and all they can talk about is dogs!"

"It killed Chunder's hens," I said.

"What did?" said Dad.

"I dunno . . ."

Dad grabbed his jacket off the chair.

"Where are you going, Dad?"

"Out!" Dad yelled. "Out! Out! Out!" and he slammed the door behind him. I don't usually wait up for Dad when he's in a rough mood, but that night I did. The wind was howling and growling down Long Moor Lane – a wind that came off the moors, prowling round the streets. You could hear it, but if you kept on listening you fancied you could hear something else. Prowling and growling. It was only the wind. It was only the wind. But I stayed on the stairs until I heard his key in the latch, and him singing, and when he was in bed I crept downstairs to make sure the front door hadn't been left open. It had, and there was a pair of yellow eyes blinking at me on the door-step.

I couldn't even yell. I just slammed the door on them – and saw, in the same second, that it was only a cat. A little cat with a pink mewing mouth, wanting a home for the night and somewhere warm to sleep and something to eat in the morning. But I didn't let it in.

The weather got better after that – not warm, but bright and stony in the daytime, and lots of glittering stars and milder frost at night. You could see Stone Cross chimney every day for a week – but it didn't look the same any more. It still looked as clear as a finger stuck up in front of your face, but it was a middle finger now, shoved up. "Up yours!" it said.

There were two lots of talking going on in Long Moor Lane. The adults talked about the mill and redundancy and poor Jim Dalton (who was getting better, so they said) and the kids talked about the Haverston Beast. Well, mostly Mick and me talked about it, and sometimes Chunder did, because of his hens and that.

So it comes near the end of March. And then comes the worst row of all – at tea time. It goes something like this.

"What have you done today?" says Dad.

"This and that," says Chunder, getting ready to go to Kirkby Haverston to strike some deal about his stud-cock.

"This and that!" says Dad. "You expecting to live on this and that for the rest of your three-score and ten?"

"I'll manage," says Chunder.

"Oh aye! You'll manage. You'll take the bread and butter out of my lad's mouth to manage, you will! And never a trip to the post office! Never a nose inside job centre!"

"I pay my way!" yells Chunder. "Who says I don't! And what bloody good has it done thee, lad? Eh? What bloody good has it done thee, walking streets, begging for a job? You tell me that?"

"At least I'm not sitting on my fat backside expecting others to feed me!" yells Dad. "At least I'm looking for work!"

"Work!" yells Chunder. "I wouldn't pay thee in brass-washers! I've got more skills in me little toe than tha's got in thee idle corpse!"

That was just the beginning. It went on, and on, and on. It was a clean fight and even-stevens matched. But it was the worst row because neither of them could win, and neither of them could lose, and nothing they yelled either way would make a fat bit of difference to the state they were in.

Then Dad yells he's going to Aberdeen to look for work, to the oil and the North Sea rigs. He's not going to sit around waiting for someone to bury him! He's going to Scotland!

And Chunder yells, "Go! Go, go, go! See what good it does yer! Go if yer like!"

And, suddenly, I know that's what Dad has been wanting him to yell – like permission, like an OK from Chunder.

But it's not OK with me.

"You can't," I said.

"Shut up!" said Dad.

"Keep out of this, Bill!" says Chunder.

"But you can't go – unless I go too."

"Don't be daft," says Dad. "You can stay here with Chunder till I get settled."

"I'm not staying with him!" I said.

"That's what you think," says Chunder. "You'll do as you're told. You'll do as your dad tells you, Bill Coward, or you'll have me to answer to!"

That's it then. They've ganged up and agreed. Maybe if I'd kept my mouth shut, they wouldn't have. But I didn't, and they did.

I started rowing with both of them, but they went so reasonable, so sensible and so reasonable it was like a plot. It was like I'd been framed. It made my blood run cold. Nothing I said would make any difference, and it damn near broke my heart. That's why it was the worst row, because come morning, Dad's bag was packed and a couple of carrier-bags. And it damn near froze my heart. Nothing I said made any difference – and, by the time I got home from school, Dad was gone.

Chunder said, "I'm sorry, Billy."

And I said, "Go to hell you," which is the only time I remember swearing at my grandad, and I didn't talk to him for a long time after that.

Oggy said, "He's right, Bill. Scotland isn't the end of the world. Some lad's fathers are going to Germany, and to the Middle East. It's the new gold rush – oil. Perhaps your dad'll strike lucky! Come home in a Rollo, eh?"

I didn't say anything. Usually Oggy and me have a crack at each other. But I didn't say anything. I couldn't think of nothing, except going home and me dad not being there . . .

I was standing up on the moors on this pointed little rise called Sparrow's Neb, watching the sun go down behind me. I mean, that was what the sun was doing, and I was watching the shadows creep across Haverston and the valley, and the colours of Stone Cross chimney changing to black. Just standing and thinking, and not wanting to go home. I hadn't bothered going to school that day. The smoke from all the chimneys on Long Moor Lane was bending sideways. The coldness had got right into my guts – coldness and emptiness, thinking of Dad and that. And why hadn't he sent me a postcard?

I'd been watching this little stick-figure come through the allotments and climb over the fence. Watching and not watching, as it climbed up towards me. It was Mick.

"What you doing up here?" he said, puffing a bit from the climb.

I shrugged.

"The Beast'll get yer!" said Mick, looking round the moor. I turned to look as well. The sun was right on the edge of the moor, like a red ball, and Aggerton Moss (which is the stretch of moor between Haverston and Kirkby Haverston) was as red as rust. There was nothing alive to see – not even a sheep or a bird flying. But then Aggerton Moss is mostly marshy bog and peat, and the only safe place to cross it is by the road. A thin black line across the rusty red.

"You going to stay up here all night, or what?" said Mick.

"No. I was just thinking."

"About your dad?"

I didn't say anything. Thinking about Dad was private.

"I saw you from the street," said Mick. "You looked like one of those Aztecs with the sun behind you."

We started walking down.

"If you won five hundred pounds, would your dad come back from Scotland?" said Mick.

I made a noise like a laugh. I wasn't in the mood for talking about stupid things like that.

"No, really," said Mick, as we squeezed through the fence and got back onto the street. "If you won five hundred . . . "

"Ah, shut up, Micky!" I said.

"Oh!" said Mick. "If you don't want to hear about it, I shan't tell you!"

"Tell me what?"

"About this five hundred pound reward."

"What five hundred pound reward?"

"The one I was telling you about until you told me to shut up," said Mick, grinning his head off.

I could have belted him, but I didn't. "Well, go on. Tell us then."

"Let's go round your place," said Mick. "It's too blooming cold to stand round here."

He was right. I could feel my teeth chattering.

"Evening, Mr Coward," said Mick when we went in.

"Oh, hello Mick," said Chunder. "What's for tea, our Billy?"

"How should I know," I said, and me and Mick went upstairs to my bedroom.

"You and Chunder fallen out or something?" said Mick.

"No. We're just not talking!"

That made Mick laugh, and after a bit it made me laugh as well. The light bulb had gone in my room, so I got a candle stub and put it in the neck of a Newcastle Brown bottle to hold it. It looked quite good, like those posh restaurants. "Steak and chips for two," I said, and tucked my sheet into my jumper like a serviette – but Mick didn't get it.

"Listen," he said, pulling this folded piece of newspaper out of his back pocket. "They're offering a five hundred pound reward for a picture of the Haverston Beast."

"Geron!" I said. "Give us a read."

"It says here," said Mick, "that a local business man, who wishes to remain anonymous, is offering five hundred pounds reward to anyone who can put an end to the rumours that are circulating in the town. He told the *Gazette* that he was sick and tired of this nonsense. 'It's giving a bad name to the area, and unless a stop is put to this nonsense it will frighten tourists away. The town has had enough bad publicity recently due to the redundancies and strikes. It's about time local people started thinking in a responsible way about the future of this area.' He added, 'Of course, the farmers are having problems, and I sympathise with them. But these foolish rumours must be nipped in the bud, or the rest of the country will think we are a superstitious backwater. Industrialists will not want to bring new factories to such a place. I have even heard people saying that the devil is on the loose! And my own children are afraid to walk home from school because of the things they have heard about the so-called Haverston Beast. I am willing to pay five hundred pounds to the farmer that rids us of this sheep-killer, or to anyone who can show me a photograph or otherwise prove that this so-called Haverston Beast is something other than a dog!'"

"Well," said Mick, "How about it?"

"How about what?"

"You and me taking a picture of it!"

"We haven't even got a camera," I said.

Mick was quiet for a moment. "I know who has – Oggy."

"And what's he going to do? Lend it to us? Oh aye, Oggy's full of tricks like that!"

"We could *borrow* it," said Mick slowly. "Out of his car – when he's not looking . . . And we'd put it back afterwards . . . Just borrow it. Not nick it or owt like that . . . " He was looking at me across the candle flame. His face was the same colour as Aggerton Moss, and his eyes were full of bright shadows. "Well?"

"I dunno . . . He'd kill us if he found out . . . "

"He wouldn't find out! And, anyway, we could give him some of the money – a fiver or something for the loan . . . "

"I dunno . . . " I said again.

"You could keep the rest of the money – maybe I'd keep twenty pounds," said Mick. He did a quick muttering sum. "That'd leave four hundred and fifty – I mean, four hundred and seventy-five pounds for you. You could buy some new hens for Chunder! And your dad would come home!"

"What would you get out of it, then?"

"It would just show them!" Mick said softly. "It would just show them!" And I knew he was talking about the kids at school who went on about his dad being in the loony bin.

"Well?" said Mick.

"Maybe . . . " I said.

"Great!" said Mick.

With friends like Mick, who needs enemies?

# Chapter 7

It wasn't all Mick's fault. I was pretty fed up and in a mood to do anything.

The next day, being Saturday, there wasn't much we could do, although I had an idea. I went round to Mick's to see if his mam had a map, a large-scale one of the area. She had.

"What do you want that for?" said Mick. We took it up to his bedroom and spread it out on the floor.

"Lend us a pencil," I said. "I want to mark on the map all the places where people have seen the Beast – all the reports. Then we'll have some idea where to look."

"I was just thinking of doing that when you came," said Mick, lying his head off. But he went downstairs and got all the recent copies of the *Gazette* he could lay his hands on.

It took quite a while to do – to find places and that.

"Peter Hargreaves said he'd seen the Beast down by the canal," said Mick, "and Sean Ashley reckoned he'd seen it over East Haverston way . . . "

"I'm not marking them down!" I said. "They just made that up. I mean, you said you'd seen it out of your bedroom window! D'you expect me to mark that down?"

Mick went red. "Well, maybe, maybe not. It might have been the Beast – but I only caught a glimpse of it . . . "

I didn't push it. On the map we had about nine crosses and seven question marks (like the one over Kirkby Haverston church, where Martin Clough said the claw prints had led from). And if you looked at them, and looked at the dates, it was like a trail leading from the allotments up over Aggerton Moss to Crag Cottage, down to Hardale, along that valley to Kirkby Haverston and then back to Hardale. All the recent sheep scares had been round Hardale . . .

"It looks like the Beast came out of town . . ." said Mick. "I wonder where it came from?"

"It might just be a dog," I said.

"Did a dog kill Chunder's hens?" said Mick. We looked at each other, then back at the map.

"So," said Mick, sounding like a TV detective, "we know it's black. It's big enough to tackle a ram, and it's somewhere over Hardale way. It's not a lot to go on."

"It could be two dogs," I said, and went off into Haverston on the bus to do some shopping. Nothing special. Just food.

When I got home, Chunder was sitting with his face in his hands, crying very very quietly.

"What's to do?" I said, dumping the carrier-bag on the table.

"Nowt," said Chunder. "Bugger off."

"Well, it's a nowt that's making you cry, Chunder," I said. I thought maybe he was ill, or that something had happened to my dad. (I tried not to think that, but you can't help it.)

"Bugger off," said Chunder, wiping his face on his sleeve. So I went and stood next to him, and I put my hand on his arm, like Dad did that day when they couldn't see Stone Cross chimney.

He patted my hand. "You talking to me again then, our Billy?"

"I suppose so."

"Good lad."

"Is that what you were crying about?"

"Maybe. That and other things. It's funny Ned not being here . . . And just sitting around all day waiting to be carried out feet first . . . "

"Eh up, Chunder! You're going soft in the head!"

Chunder just smiled. "What's fer tea?"

"Hot-pot."

"Got any red cabbage to go with it?"

"Aye."

"Grand as owt," said Chunder. "I'll peel the spuds."

On Monday afternoon we stole Oggy's camera. Mick was having himself on, saying it was borrowing. As far as Oggy and the law were concerned, I reckon, until we gave it back, it was nicking. I mean, can you imagine anyone believing us if we'd said we'd just borrowed it?

This is how we did it. At home time we hung around until we saw Oggy unlock his car and dump his black bag and his camera gear in the back seat, then Mick rushed out and attacked this lad. It just happened to be Peter Hargreaves. He wasn't expecting to be jumped on, so he fell over, and Mick starts thumping him and yelling at the top of his voice, "If you call my dad that again, I'll kill you, Hargreaves!"

Hargreaves deserved it, because he had been saying things about Mick's dad, even though he hadn't been saying anything on that Monday.

Well, Oggy goes charging up to separate them, and I nip round the corner and lift his camera off the seat. Nothing else. Not his bag of equipment or owt. I shoved it in my jacket, and ran for the bus. I landed on the platform just as it was moving, and I got a mouthful off the conductor, but nothing like the mouthful Peter Hargreaves and Mick were getting off Oggy.

To tell the truth, I felt pretty bad about it, even though we did mean to get the camera back to him in the end. Oggy and I got on OK. It didn't seem fair on him.

Well, so there we were, round at my house that night, when we hit our first big problem. Neither of us knew how to use the damn thing! Mick kept licking his split lip and saying, "Try pressing that. Perhaps its batteries are flat," and other daft comments.

"Wait on, wait on," I said. I tried to think of someone who

took pictures. Then it struck me. Danny at the fish and chip shop had all these photographs on his notice board of his holiday in Majorca.

So we took the camera round to Danny's.

I told him my dad had sent me the camera from Scotland, but there weren't any instructions and could he tell us how to use it?

Danny was pleased as punch. I reckon he fancies himself as a bit of an expert, so he was really proud to show off.

"Well now, lads," he said. "Has it got a film in?"

Mick and I stared at each other.

"Oh aye," says Danny, looking at these little numbers in a dial on the top. "Looks like you've taken seven pictures already!"

"We were trying to find out how to use it," I explained.

We must have spent about an hour in the chip shop. No customers came in – partly because it was too early, and partly, Danny said, because business was a bit slack what with the redundancies and that. He explained the camera. It was complicated at first, but then Danny said, "Ah, forget about depth of field and F-stops for now," and explained it again more simply.

"I wonder what made your dad buy you a camera?" said Danny, looking at me.

"Oh," I said, "he wants me to send him some pictures of me and Chunder, and he got it cheap off this feller in Glasgow."

"Oh," said Danny, sort of winking without shutting his eye. "Reckon he was lucky to get it cheap – it's not a cheap camera, isn't this."

"What I want to know," said Mick, "is can it take pictures in the dark?"

"What do you want to take pictures in the dark for?" says Danny.

"I want to take a picture of the Haverston Beast," says Mick, bold as brass.

It was funny how the truth made Danny laugh out loud! But

he gave us these two flash-cubes and told us how to use them. Then we bought fish and chips twice even though we weren't hungry. Well, we had to really, didn't we?

Luck was on our side. Next morning we were sent home from school at assembly, because the central-heating boiler had broken down again. Mick and me made a run for it, just as a police car pulled up outside the gate.

Oggy must have told them about the stolen camera. But they came too late that day.

We didn't have any excuses left for not going. We had the camera and the map, and the day to ourselves, and I had more than enough money for the bus fare to Kirkby Haverston because of those two fivers Dad and Chunder had given me for my birthday.

It was a grey sort of day – not raining, but just a bit of cold drizzle, and these blue and yellow Jacob's Ladders streaking down the sky over the moors. On the bus we had a row about who should take the pictures. Mick won because he said it was his idea in the first place, and, besides, he wasn't going to make any money out of it – only twenty quid.

It's strange when you think about it. It was like a game we were playing. We'd gone about it very seriously, but it was still a game; even though I'd seen Chunder's hens I still didn't really believe in the Beast. I mean, I believed in it in the dark at night, but not in the daytime on a bus. Mick said we should have brought some bait – some bones or meat from the butchers. It never occurred to us then, that *we* might be all the bait we needed . . .

It was daft really, the way we set off, as if all we had to do was get off the bus at Kirkby Haverston, climb up Hardale, and there it would be, posing in a bikini for us to take a holiday snap!

It wasn't like that. It wasn't like that at all.

We followed these signs from the village, BRIDLE TRACK. HARDALE 3½. It was a long bloody three and a half miles – straight up the side of this fell, along by a dry-stone wall, then down the other side and over a wide beck. We tried to jump it, but we both landed in the water. You could see there were stepping-stones under the water, but with all the rain and snow flooding down, they were no use to us.

And then, suddenly, there's no more green path. Just steep black rocks with clouds covering the tops, and patches of twisted grey-looking trees and boggy black peat. No birds. Nothing. Only a few sheep bleating somewhere and the sound of water, rushing and hissing and trickling round the rocks and gulleys. And there's the ruins of a little house – nothing but the chimney stack and the walls only up to your knee, all built of grey stone. A house that had tumbled down hundreds of years back, it looked like.

You could imagine the Beast roaming about in this wild wasted place, lapping the water in the beck, washing the blood off its teeth, licking its claws, watching us, hidden in the rocks, or among those black twisted trees.

"Now what?" said Mick.

We were both cold and wet through – Mick even more than me, because he was only wearing trainers. I had my boots on. And I suppose we were both, suddenly, nervous.

"You got the camera ready?"

"Yes," says Mick.

But we didn't move.

We were in the mouth of Hardale valley (and it was like a mouth, a black mouth with jagged rocks for teeth) and I think both of us wanted to say, 'Let's go back', but neither of us wanted to be the first to say it.

I said, "Let's have something to eat and look at the map."

"OK," says Mick, quickly.

We went and sat in this ruined house. Funny how we did that, when you think about it. There were loads of rocks to sit on, but we went and sat in this ruin as if it had invisible ghost walls and a roof to keep us warm and safe, even though it didn't. A crow flew up the valley, going "Caah! Caark!" and vanished into the clouds. After it had gone, it felt like the silence was watching us.

Well, we ate our way through both packets of biscuits Mick had swiped from home. One after the other, very slowly, we ate them, not because we were hungry but because we just wanted an excuse to stay where we were.

Mick says, "Looks like it's going to start raining."

And I think, great! Then we'll have to go back. I don't mind admitting it – I was nervous. Not scared to death or owt. Nervous.

Every time we heard a sheep we both glanced round, even though the sound was far away – probably the farmers had all their sheep safely tucked up in Kirkby Haverston.

We didn't talk about the Beast at all. We talked about Stone Cross and our dads. Anything and everything but the Beast.

Mick said the doctors had found that his dad was probably a diabetic, and it was something to do with sugar in his blood that had made him go off his rocker. And he and his mam were very pleased that his old feller was poorly and not just mental – which is not to say anything about the poor sods who do have nervous breakdowns. It's just that they could give these injections to his dad to make him better, and they can't so easily give injections to folk who go off their rocker, apart from to keep them from hurting themselves.

"As long as he doesn't eat biscuits and doesn't drink beer, and gives himself these injections every day, he'll be all right," says Mick, scraping brown old moss off a stone with his fingernail.

So we talked about what it must be like having to stick a needle in yourself every day for the rest of your life. And Mick was just saying that it was better than going mental, when it really does start to rain.

Buckets! It pelted down, as sudden as spitting! You could see the lines the rain made in the air – it came down that hard!

We made a dash for this big rock with a kind of overhanging ledge, and crouched under it. We couldn't have walked back in that rain. You couldn't even see the beck any more – though you could hear it hissing.

We got really fed up then. There was nothing left to eat. We were wet to the skin and freezing cold, and it made you ache all over, crouched and cramped like that. And the worst thing was – it was going dark.

In the end, even though it was still raining, we had to make a run for it, because we would have died of exposure otherwise. It was horrible. Mick lost one of his trainers in this peaty bog, and I had to hold onto him while he got it out. It stank.

Then we thought we'd got lost. And I had to put the camera in my jacket because Mick's wasn't waterproof, which meant I couldn't button it up to the top, and the rain started going down my neck.

We found a wall going down a steep fell, and hoped like hell it was the right one. Somewhere we could see a light.

But it wasn't the right wall, because there started to be brambles and bushes growing by it, and there weren't any when we went up.

"We're lost!" says Mick, huddled in the rain and the darkness.

"I know!" I yelled.

"Well, you've got the sodding map!"

I pulled the map out of my pocket. It was soft and limp as a dishcloth, and anyway it was too dark to see it properly. Trying to look at the map made us realise how dark it was. But we tried to find out where we were all the same. It was plain bloody crazy. But that's what we were doing, when suddenly I hear this noise. I grabbed Mick's shoulder to stop him arguing, and his back went stiff under my hand – hard as metal. He'd heard it too.

It was a soft crunching noise, over in the brambles and bushes. The sort of noise a big dog makes when it's chewing a bone. A scraping, soft grinding, and a bit of rustling.

We froze solid. It was the Beast. We both knew it was the Beast – not posing for a picture on a bright sunny day, but eating something it had killed in the dark and rainy bushes.

The wind was blowing the rain in our faces, and the Beast was down the hill from us. It must have heard us – but maybe it hadn't smelled us.

There was a sort of contented growly noise, then the scraping of teeth again, and more rustling.

You wouldn't believe how fast your mind works when you think you're going to be killed . . . I remember thinking we were both going to have our throats torn out, and someone would find our bodies, and nobody would know what had done it until they found the camera and the last pictures we'd taken . . .

I pulled the camera out of my jacket. I could hear every instruction Danny had given us as clear as if he was standing behind me. I even remembered to take off the lens cover. It was like a gun without the sound. A bullet of light.

One flash, and we saw a pair of red eyes, a hunched black shape among bushes and brambles. Then pitch black, and the crash of twigs and branches as the Beast hurtled out of the bushes towards us. Past us! Another great flash, and a glimpse of something big and black leaping the wall, with a long thin tail streaming behind, balancing it. Then pitch black. Black silence.

We ran.

We burst into the public bar of *The Cocks*, knocked over a game of dominoes, almost got speared by flying darts, and landed up against the pool table, panting and gulping.

That wall we'd followed was the wrong wall, but it had led us onto Kirkby Harverston main street.

All these old lads were gawping at us, and the landlord ducked under the bar, ready to throw us out. I shoved the camera back into my jacket.

"What's all this?" says the landlord.

Then a voice says, "It's Charlie Coward's grandson, isn't it?" It was Bill Howgill. "What's to do wi' you, lad?"

"We got lost," I said (well, gasped and grunted), "looking for Chunder. Got lost."

"Eh, you're soaked through!" says Bill Howgill, as if we didn't know.

Anyhow, to cut a long story short. It was only about half past seven. Old Bill gave us a lift back to Haverston because the last bus had gone, and neither Mick nor me said a word about what we had seen. Partly because we were in possession of a stolen camera, and partly because there was nothing to say.

But we had the pictures. And we hadn't had our throats ripped out.

It didn't seem real the next day. It was like being drunk. Real and not real. Like dreaming. Except we had the camera and the pictures, and Mick got into a lot of trouble from his mam for coming in like that – covered in mud and soaking. I suppose she had enough to worry about without having to worry about him and all.

Chunder was that pleased to see old Bill Howgill that he soon forgot about me.

All night it was like a dream – sleeping a bit, then waking up in the dark, sometimes scared and sometimes thinking about the five hundred pounds . . .

All the time, in my mind, clear as a photograph and yet drunk-blurred, I could see the Beast leaping over that wall. I knew what it was, and yet I didn't know what it was. One thing I knew – it wasn't a dog. Or at least, no dog I'd ever seen.

Once in the night I dreamed it was a cow, and everyone was laughing at us. Mick and me were in jail for stealing the camera and everyone paid money to come and laugh at us, and there were free tickets for people on the dole!

Next morning took ages to come, and as you can imagine, Mick and me were in town even before the shops were open, wanting to get this film turned into pictures. The first place we tried was useless. It was a flashy camera shop. We asked the man to take the film out of the camera because we didn't know how. He did that, but then he said it would be five days before we got the prints!

"Can't you do it today?" says Mick.

The man just laughed, and said he had to send it off to a place to be done. But we couldn't wait that long. One reason being that someone else might get a picture to the *Gazette* before us, and the other reason being that until we actually saw the pictures it would still be like a dream. It wouldn't be real until then. And we had to know – one way or the other – whether to be scared or not. Long-term scared, not just panicked.

I asked him if there wasn't someone who could do it for us while-U-wait. Then Mick has this brainwave, and says my dad's going to Saudi tomorrow and we want to give him the pictures of the family to take with him.

"Going to look for work?" says the man.

Mick nodded.

Then the man says, "Well . . . Old Mr Dickson at the chemist . . . He's got a dark-room. Used to do all his work on the premises . . . I can't promise . . . "

"Dickson's on Mill Street?"

"Yes. That's the one. It's only black and white, mind . . . "

We were gone, and the man was yelling, "Good luck!" and shaking his head at us.

Dickson looked like a skeleton, a yellow skeleton with two candles in its eyes. And it's a dark old shop, like something out of the olden days – full of tonic wines and tooth powder and cures for sheep ticks. It had a smell like medicinal soap and the shampoo you use when you get nits. When we went in, we both thought it was going to end up a wild goose chase. But Mick tells the skeleton his story, and the skeleton rattles and ums and haws a bit, and then he says he'll do it!

He disappeared into the back of the shop, and Mick and me waited on these wooden chairs.

Mick said, thoughtfully, "We could raid the till. He'd never know."

I jabbed him in the ribs with my elbow and he collapsed on the floor, half dying and half laughing.

Through Dickson's windows you could see the gates of Stone Cross, and there was yellow cellophane across the bottoms of his windows to stop things fading. Looking at Stone Cross through that was like looking at an old-fashioned photograph of the mill. The people walking by, and the gates and the shadows looked yellow and brown. And the people at the bus stop looked as though they were queuing for a job at the mill – like they did in the olden days. I tried to tell Mick about it, but he wasn't interested.

It took ages.

Mick nicked a tin of boiled sweets off the counter. They tasted horrible, but we ate them. Then he pretended to be a reporter (using a gent's hair-brush as a microphone):

"Tell me, Mr Coward, did you, or did you not, see the Haverston Beast?"

"I dunno," I said. "Did you?"

"Yes," said Mick. "Oh, yes, I saw it."

About dinner time, the skeleton came out of the dark-room.

"What did you say these pictures were of?" he said.

Mick and I said nothing.

"You realise half the film was blank?"

We nodded.

The skeleton made these rattling sounds in his chest – I suppose he was coughing. "There's a picture here, I wouldn't mind having a copy of," says the skeleton. "It's a pity about these last two . . ."

"They're ours!" says Mick.

Mr Dickson handed over the negatives and eight photos and kept one in his hand.

They were black and white. They were Stone Cross, in the

dark – pickets and police and the chimney half lit up. Apart from one that was just grey splodges and another that was just blurred shapes, black and white.

Mick yells, "Give us that photo!" because Dickson is still holding this last one.

The skeleton handed it over. It was four faces, men's faces, staring up at the chimney of Stone Cross, with shadows deep as scars in the lines under their eyes.

"That'll be three pounds thirty-two," says the skeleton.

But where's the picture of the Beast?

Mick goes mad – yelling at him to hand over the rest of the photos. But there aren't any. Work it out. There were seven pictures on Oggy's film when we nicked the camera, and we took two. We had nine pictures in our hands.

I gave the skeleton the money. It wasn't his fault. And they were bloody good photos of Stone Cross, taken, I reckon, on the night Oggy sat on my old feller's chest.

Mick and I stood in the bus shelter, staring and staring at them.

Then we saw the Beast.

It was on one of those blurred pictures. You had to look hard – but there it was. The shape of it, crouched over something, and two flashes of its eyes.

Once you saw it, you saw it again. And you sort of knew what it was. You knew and you didn't know.

"That's it!" yells Mick. "That's the Beast!"

And we ran, to the offices of the *Haverston Gazette*.

# Chapter 8

On the way there we passed a gang of lads from our school.

"Is the boiler still broken down?" I yelled as we shot past.

"Yes!" one of them yelled back. That meant we weren't being missed from school, which was a relief.

Then another of these lads turns round. It's Peter Hargreaves. "I'm going to get you, Dalton!" he yells, and they start haring after us.

We dashed into the *Haverston Gazette* office. They didn't follow us in, but hung around on the pavement outside, waiting to get us when we came out.

The *Gazette* office is really a posh stationers. It sells wedding cards with silver bells on them, and twenty-first birthday cards in a box with a silver key, and even funeral cards with black and golden edges. It's very quiet in there, with a brown carpet and two middle-aged ladies serving. We went to the back, where there's a counter you go to if you want to put an advert into the *Gazette*.

"We want to see the boss," I said.

"The editor," said Mick, which is what I really meant.

The woman looked at us. She had glasses on with a chain that hung round her neck. "He's busy," she said. "Perhaps I can help you, boys."

"It's about the Haverston Beast," said Mick. He was clutching the photograph.

"Oh," said the woman, "it would be. He's definitely busy."

And she gave us this sour sneery look, like she was the Queen and we were something that had crawled up the Royal plughole.

There was a door to one side of the counter. You could tell just by looking at it that behind it, somewhere, was the editor's office.

"You can't go in there! Come back here this instant!" she yelled, but we were already off up the stairs.

Although the shop was so posh, the stairs and the corridors behind it looked old and grubby. You could hear machines clattering. We didn't know where we were going, but that editor's office wasn't hard to find. It was at the top of these stairs, on the right. It had a brown door with *Mr Arkwright. Editor* written on it in white letters.

We didn't knock. We just walked in. The editor wasn't busy at all – he was just reading some newspaper cuttings. He looked a bit surprised to see us though.

"Hello," I said.

"What . . . " said Mr Arkwright, standing up and staring at us.

"We've come to see you!" says Mick. "It's important!"

A very thin smile came onto the man's mouth. He was a thin man in a grey suit and he had a thin smile. "Don't tell me," he said, "let me guess. It's about the Haverston Beast, yes?"

"Yes!" we both said.

"And you want to claim the five hundred pounds because you've taken a photograph of it, yes?"

"Yes!"

"And this photograph is rather blurred and out of focus because you've never used a camera before – or because the Beast was moving fast – or because it was the middle of the night, yes?"

"Yes!" For a moment I thought maybe Dickson had rung up and told him about us.

"Or maybe," said the thin smile, "it's a picture of a lion that your Uncle Sid took and that thing that looks like a palm tree is really an apple tree your Aunty Maud pruned that way, yes?"

"No," I said. I took the picture from Mick and held it out to him.

He didn't even glance at it. "On your bikes, lads," he said. "I've had enough jokers already."

"This isn't a joke!" said Mick, staring at him. "We took the pictures in Kirkby Haverston. We went up Hardale – it nearly bloody got us! Last night!"

"Go on. Hop it," said the editor.

"Are you blooming deaf or what?" I said. I didn't shout. The room was filling with cool grey smoke, and I could see silky blue flames at the edges of my eyes and I could feel a cold blue flame, like ice, in my belly.

"Out," said the editor. "Stop wasting my time. And close the door behind you."

You know I said at the beginning of all this that there was a thread. Well, I think maybe it wasn't so much a thread as a fuse. A long slow-burning fuse that was lit the day Chunder and Dad stood at the window looking for the chimney. A fuse that had quietly fizzed and smoked away until, in the editor's office, it reached the case of dynamite – me.

"Look! Look!" I yelled, quite softly, shoving the photograph under his nose. "Are you blind as well as being deaf and daft?"

The thin man backed away, but I followed him, shoving the photo at him, trying to make him look at it, and calling him everything I could think of. It wasn't just the five hundred pounds, it was that stupid thin smile and not being believed.

I was yelling, "What the hell's up with yer?" and I knocked some of the papers off his desk, when Mick grabbed me by the arm and dragged me out.

"Leave it!" Mick was yelling, and trying to drag me out of the shop. "Leave it alone, will yer!"

The only good thing I can say about that day is that Peter Hargreaves and his gang had got fed up of hanging round and had gone. It was a good thing too. I was in the mood to kill someone, and Hargreaves would have done just as nicely as anyone else.

The editor was staring at us out of his office window, and the two women were glaring at us out of the shop window.

"You wait!" I yelled at him. "You just sodding wait! I'll show yer! Even if I've got to drag the bloody Beast here by its tail!" And I screwed up that photo – that precious photo we'd stolen a camera, got soaked to the skin and nearly got our throats ripped out to get. I screwed it up and threw it at the thin face in the window, and then I grabbed the rest of the pictures and negatives off Mick and lugged them as well.

I think I would have thrown the camera through the window – except Mick had run off down the street carrying it, which was a good thing I suppose.

I followed him. I was seething. That's what it felt like – seething and burning like hot ice and freezing flames.

I caught up with Mick halfway up the hill, heading for Long Moor Lane. He looked very white. "You're flaming crazy, Bill Coward!" he kept saying. "You needn't have done that!"

But now the smoke was clearing, and only one steady flame was left burning in my guts. I trudged along beside him.

"We'll have to get this camera back to Oggy," he said.

"Sod it! You get it back to him!" I said.

"How?" said Mick.

"How the hell should I know!"

"What are you going to do?"

"I dunno . . . Something! I'm going to do something!"

"You didn't really mean it, did you? About catching the Beast?" said Mick, stopping and gawping at me like I'd gone mental.

I didn't answer, because that's just what I was going to do.

"Count me out," says Mick, softly. "Count me out, that's all!"

"I never counted you in, in the first place, Mick Dalton," I said, and left him standing there.

I didn't go home. I went up to Sparrow's Neb and crouched there, staring down at Haverston. No, not staring – but glaring. I've never felt so much anger and hate before in my life. It felt as if it was concentrated in my eyes, and they were like laser-beams, and just by staring at streets and buildings and people I could blow them off the face of the earth.

First, Stone Cross chimney collapsed across Mill Street in a pile of rubble, then the gas-works exploded in a ball of flame, then all the windows shattered on Laurel Ridge estate and the roofs fell in. Then a great crack appeared along High Street – cars and buses were swallowed up, and the offices of the *Haverston Gazette* crumpled and slid down it.

But, of course, nothing happened. No one noticed. Haverston didn't look up. You can hardly blame them. There was nothing to see – only Bill Coward crouched on Sparrow's Neb in the rain.

But at that moment I wished I was an alien with the power to blast the whole of my town to bits. And, a moment later, I wished I was the Beast. I had a picture in my mind of what it would feel like prowling along High Street in broad daylight, with people screaming and grabbing their kids and running for the shop doors. I, the Beast, clearing the streets just by walking down them, and maybe Dad and Chunder would be walking along behind me – the only two who weren't afraid . . .

Funny, isn't it? There was me, planning to hunt the Beast, and wanting to be the Beast all at the same time. I suppose I was wanting, just for once in my life, to be something so powerful and scary that people would take notice. Wanting not just to be another kid on Long Moor Lane whose old feller and grandad got pushed around, and who would get pushed around in the end as well. School, dole queue, maybe even

111

another Stone Cross if I was lucky . . . I'd rather be the Beast any day, I can tell you.

I was so mad that I didn't hardly notice the rain – not even when it stopped. But at last I stood up, my legs as stiff as broomsticks, and I turned round to look at the moor. Would you believe it? There was a rainbow over Aggerton Moss.

I think I hated that rainbow more than anything else in the world – just for looking so beautiful, and for it all being lies what they tell you about the pots of gold and that.

If you've never been in a temper like that, I expect it would be very hard to guess what it feels like. Just because I'd stopped shouting outside the *Gazette* office didn't mean I'd calmed down. It was worse than that. I felt calm all right, calm and cold and seeing everything very clear and sharp. I expect you could plan a really complicated murder in a mood like that – calm and cold as that – and the judge would call it a cold-blooded killing, not knowing that you were in the worst temper any one could be in. A cold-blooded temper, cold as ice, planning things clear and cold as new glass.

I dunno. I can't explain. Once it's gone it's hard to remember and hard to explain. It's not like losing your rag. It's not like the blue touch-paper brigade. You don't need to shout and you don't need to swear, because you're too busy planning – and it can go on for days. Days and days. As long as it needs to. And, all the while, you just go about doing ordinary things.

I went home and made tea, egg and chips, for Chunder and me.

Chunder shoved a letter into his pocket as I came in. Something he didn't want me to see. I thought (with the bit of my brain that was still working in the ordinary way) that maybe it was something to do with his stud cock, but it made me think of Dad and all.

"Wonder why Dad hasn't sent us a postcard?" I said as we ate tea.

"Oh, he's going to, lad," said Chunder with his gob full of chips.

"What do you mean – he's going to? How do you know?"

Chunder coughed and spluttered, pretending he'd got a chip down his wind pipe.

"I mean to say, he will," he said quickly. "You know – when he's got something to tell us, like."

I felt a bit suspicious, but my mind was too full of other things to bother about it just then.

After tea I left Chunder to watch *This is your Right* on the telly, and I went up to the allotment to sit in the shed and plan.

That was where the Beast had first struck, so it seemed the only place to go and think about it.

It was very quiet up there – lonely, without Chunder's old hens pecking about and nagging at each other. The hen enclosure looked like an empty cage, but it wasn't a cage I needed – it was a gun.

I sat staring at the place on the barbed-wire where that tuft of fur had been until it went dark, and a picture kept flashing in my mind, blurred and dim, of the Beast leaping over the wall in the rain. And that feeling that I knew what it was, was stronger than ever. It was like trying to remember something – it was on the tip of my tongue, but I couldn't just spit it out.

So I sat in the doorway of the shed, with night coming on, smoking one of Chunder's fags, and trying to work out how I could get a gun. On the telly there's always a gun lying round when someone wants one, but mostly the programmes are American. It's not like that in Long Moor Lane.

I hadn't got that kind of money, and I hadn't got a licence. All I'd got was my stupid air-rifle and three tins of slugs. Well, an air-rifle like mine is all right for cans and sparrows, even for the occasional rabbit and pigeon, long as you're close enough. But it wouldn't be much use for a duck, let alone a dog. You'd wing them, but you'd probably not kill them. It's not the sort of thing you'd go hunting a Beast with. I mean, you'd really need a shotgun for ducks, like the wildfowlers use – at least the young ones – but for a big dog, to stop a big Alsatian dead in its tracks, you'd be best with .22 or something like that, I reckon.

I sat thinking, with my chin on my hands, and I bet I had more wrinkles on my face than even our Chunder – I was thinking that hard!

I knew some of Chunder's old mates up Kirkby Haverston had guns – but they'd not lend them to me, and the only other place I knew was Hamnet Lord and Sons. They had cases and cases of them. It made me seethe, thinking of the shop empty at night, and all those guns and rifles . . . But I was mad, not mental. I knew I'd never stand a chance trying to break in. They've got more alarms than Fort Knox on a shop like that.

Or maybe I was mental. Because thinking about Hamnet Lord and Sons made me remember that old feller who'd bought the slugs for me. So, all right, he was buying fishing tackle at the time but he must have known something about guns, even to get those slugs for me. And he seemed like gentry, and where there's gentry there's shooters – the hunting, shooting and fishing brigade, Dad calls them. And, even more important, he seemed like a really nice old gent who was fed up of having a nit for a grandson . . . Only trouble was – I didn't even know his name. But I knew where I could find out, because he asked Mr Hamnet to deliver, didn't he? So I reckoned he must have been an old customer, a regular as you might say.

Well, there was nothing I could do that night, so I went home. I still had the map in my jacket pocket. It was very damp, but I spread it out on my bedroom floor, lit my candle (I don't know why I hadn't bought a new light bulb. Since Dad had gone, things like that seemed to have got forgotten somehow . . . ) and spent a long time looking at it. I tried to remember where streams went and that, and where those pointy grass symbols were which meant marshy bog. Aggerton Moss was covered in those.

I knew it would be different in real life than it was on the map, but I did my best. I didn't bother with the names of places or owt – just which way the streams ran and where they went. And they all went into Aggerton Moss and then down the valley into the river, except for a few which went to Kirkby Haverston and joined the river up there.

And I'll tell you a funny thing. By the time I went to bed that night, I wasn't thinking about Mr Arkwright and his thin smile anymore, or about the five hundred quid, or even about showing the sods. I was just thinking about the Beast and nothing else.

That night I had my last dream about it. I dreamed *I* was the Beast. I knew I was, in a sort of dream way, because I was a pair of yellow eyes, like laser-beams, staring and staring through the darkness at the chimney of Stone Cross Mill. And, at last, the chimney fell . . .

First thing next morning I went to Hamnet Lord and Sons. It was a bright clear day. Everything had a hard edge to it – maybe that was the weather or maybe it was just my mood. I don't know.

Anyway, I went in. I love that shop – it's got everything in it. Knives, decoys, boots, guns, lines, ferret harnesses, nets – you name it. If ever I won the pools I'd buy a shop like that.

"You again?" says Mr Hamnet. "What is it this time? Targets? Slugs? An ounce of maggots?" He said it sarky like, but he was smiling at me. He doesn't really mind me, Mr Hamnet doesn't. It's Mr Lord I have to watch out for. He's got it into his head that I pinch things, but I swear God's Honest Truth I never have done, not from there.

I said, "Mr Hamnet, you know when I come in last? There was an old feller bought some slugs for me?"

"Don't look a gift horse in the mouth," says Mr Hamnet. "And don't try pushing your luck, sonny."

"I'm not," I said. "I just wanted to know who he was. I wanted to say thanks, that's all."

"Pull the other one," says Mr Hamnet, leaning on the counter. It's a lovely counter – wood polished so you can see your face in it.

I thought quick. "Well," I says, "I do want to say thanks. And me dad wants to know who got them for me – he reckons I nicked them!"

"Ah," says Mr Hamnet, "now we're getting at the truth."

Isn't it funny how he believed that? Sometimes I think people have got wrong impressions of me and dad.

"Well," says Mr Hamnet. "That was Major Farlton-Smith, that was. He's an old customer of mine. Don't you go pestering him – or I'll have your guts for garters!"

"Who?" I said.

"Major Farlton-Smith, Retired, from Hardale Hall," says Mr Hamnet. "And he doesn't suffer fools lightly."

"Champion," I said, and left. But I reckoned he suffered some fools, remembering his grandson. Still, I thought luck was on my side. If he lived in Hardale, he'd know about the Beast.

I headed for the nearest phone box. The yellow pages were all ripped up but the directory was just about in one piece. It took ages to find the number because I looked under Smith. (There's loads of Smiths.) And then I had a brainwave and looked under F and found him. *Then* I had to go out and get change from the newsagent for fifty pence.

But, at last, I got through.

"Hello," I said.

"Good morning. This is the Farlton-Smith residence. Who's speaking?" says this posh voice.

And, suddenly, I couldn't say anything at all.

"Hello? Hello?" says this voice. This voice as cold and hard and shiny as the bonnet of a white Mercedes.

I just stood there, holding the phone to my ear, staring out through a broken square of glass, feeling sick with the smell of pee and fag ends in the phone box, and with my own self for being so bloody stupid. What was I going to do? Ask him if I could borrow his rifle? Stupid! Stupid! Stupid!

So I just stood there, until the man at the other end put the receiver down. I heard it click, then whirr, like an empty noise filling my head.

A copper came wandering up the street, and he slowed down when he saw me in the phone box, and peered in.

I'm not up to anything, officer, I thought to myself. Just ringing this feller to ask if I could have a lend of his gun . . .

I left the phone box then. And because that voice had been real, nothing else was. Me? Hunting the Beast? Don't make me laugh! Stupid! Stupid! Stupid!

Even the Beast wasn't real any more. Just for a minute, that voice had turned all my anger, and the Beast, into a stupid dream.

I wandered back up the hill. Thinking about nothing. There was nothing to think about any more.

But, just as I turned into Long Moor Lane, I saw something out of the corner of my eye. Do you remember that little cat that had come mewing round our doorstep one night when my dad had had a few?

It was the same cat – jumping onto a wall.

A cat. A black cat, jumping onto a wall.

Jumping over a wall.

With its tail stretched out for balance, and its body slung thin, and its haunches sharp.

A cat jumping over a wall.

Not a dog. Not two dogs.

But a cat as big as my dad.

A zoo cat.

A circus cat.

"RSPCA'll put a stop to that outfit . . . Bet they haven't even got licences for their big cats!"

# Chapter 9

I knew.

I was the only person in Haverston that knew, and I wasn't telling. How can I make you understand why I didn't tell any one? First on, there was the flame, the temper, in my guts. Second, more important, that one bit of knowing was like the only power I'd ever had. No one had given it to me and no one could take it away. It was dangerous and it was mine. It was a secret, and as long as it stayed my secret, it was my power, because whoever has the secrets has the power, I reckon.

And, thirdly, nobody would have believed me. People only seem to believe me when I'm lying – when I tell the truth they mostly laugh or ignore me.

I expect if anyone was watching me they'd have thought I'd gone stark staring bonkers! I was gawping, terrified, at this little black cat sitting on a wall, washing its whiskers. My feet wouldn't move. Nothing would move, and all the hair on the back of my head began to creep. I'm not lying. It really does stand on end, well, creep, when you're scared witless.

Or maybe I was witless already. Some folks will think I was.

I turned round, went back into town and straight to the library.

"I want a book on cats," I said.

Silly old blighter gave me a book about moggies, but it was

all right because on the same shelf I found what I was looking for. I flicked through the pages of this big book, then I closed it with a bang. Some people looked at me.

It was black.

It was a panther.

I didn't read any more. I shut the book, because the Beast was staring at me out of the page.

I recognised him, but I didn't want him to recognise me.

I don't remember walking home.

"Billy?" said Chunder. "I want to talk to you."

"Not now," I said.

"It's about your Dad . . . "

"Not NOW."

"Good enough," said Chunder, and went out to feed Betty.

This is what I did that night. I dried the map in front of the fire and put it in a plastic bag. Then I got all the food I could lay my hands on, and started packing my football bag. Food. Matches. A new dustbin liner to sleep in. Knife. A packet of Chunder's fags. And, I admit, another fiver I nicked from under his mattress. Some other things as well. I can hardly remember.

Then I went upstairs and cleaned my air-rifle.

I cleaned my air-rifle knowing that it was no better than a water-pistol. I went out after the Beast, knowing what it was, and knowing that my air-rifle was nowt. I had a feeling in my eyes like burning when I sat cleaning it. Not crying. (If I had cried I wouldn't have gone.) Just burning. Knowing it was useless, and knowing that other people, rich people, had guns – even real rifles – that they never used except for shooting stupid pheasants or the family pet when it wanted putting down . . . I don't know. I don't know what I thought. I was past thinking much at all. Perhaps it sounds like I'm boasting – blowing my mouth about how I went, single-handed, to tackle the Beast. It wasn't like that.

It didn't feel like that.

It felt like my dad would never come back home again. It felt like there wasn't any point growing up when they could do things like that at Stone Cross. It felt like it was the one thing ever, in my whole life, that was mine to do. For me. For Dad. For Chunder.

That's what it felt like most. That's why I went.

Maybe I slept. Maybe I didn't. When it got grey I left the house. Aggerton Moss was still dark, but over Haverston way there was a thin red line with some purple clouds over it. And the rest of the sky was the colour of this big sea-shell we once had in our class at junior school.

I walked half the way to Kirkby Haverston, and the rest of the way I got a lift in this milk tanker. The driver asked me to pour him some tea out of his flask. He yawned and supped his tea, and steered the tanker with one hand.

I was glad of that lift. I'd not walked that far for some time – leastways, not after not having any sleep, and my chest hurt a bit. Like a stitch, but higher up.

We talked about football, and he was smiling to himself, then he dropped me outside *The Hare and Hounds*.

The village was quiet, dead quiet. Like a ghost village. A few rooks flew up off the pub car park. A dog barked once or twice, far away. The fell sides looked as soft as cushions, with darkness in the brown creases. And the air was as cold as glass. Sharp in your nose and throat, like air no one had ever breathed before.

The air-rifle had a slug in it and it was cocked, but I didn't want to find the Beast straight off. I wanted to find somewhere where me and the Beast were more equal – well, where I had the upper hand.

And I wanted to go home. I admit it. I wanted to go home, and wake up in my bed, with Dad and Chunder rowing, and everything the same as it always used to be . . .

First, I had a look round the churchyard. The rooks were

making a racket in the tall trees and a blackbird was pecking about in the dead leaves by the hedge. It wasn't like a municipal graveyard – all terraces of crosses and slabs and angels. It was more of a garden. Small and tidy, with the leaves raked up onto the compost heap in the corner, and bunches of daffodils in vases in the graves. There were even some flowers growing – little purple ones under the hedge. They weren't quite open.

I'm not sure what I was looking for. Something useful, something I could use against the Beast, or maybe I was just putting off going up Hardale. I even went and looked inside the church. Would you believe it? The door wasn't locked!

It was very quiet and cold in there – grey stones, with red cushions to kneel on and coloured glass in the windows. I didn't touch anything. There were even postcards left out and a box to put the money in. They must be very trusting up Kirkby Haverston way – or maybe they've got video cameras hidden up in the roof, like they do in the shops. I don't know.

When I came outside again the sun was coming up. I glanced up at the sky behind the tower of the church, and noticed all these stone beasts staring down at me from above the church door. It gave me a right shock! Snarling and bog-eyed, with great big teeth and horns and tongues stuck out!

They looked as if they were laughing at me and wishing me bad luck, so I left the churchyard then.

I set off up the bridletrack. The sun was warm. I could feel it through the back of my donkey-jacket, and it was almost like Spring. Snowdrops in the gardens, a couple of lambs in the field behind *The Cocks*. I even saw a hare zig-zagging away up the fell – but I didn't take a crack at it.

Once I'd set off I began to feel sort of happy, hard and happy. I had the air-rifle slung over my shoulder, and the stitch had almost gone. I might have whistled but I was chewing the end of a match. Walking along, I almost forgot about the Beast. It was just a good feeling. If I win the pools, after buying a gunsmith's shop, I'll spend the rest on a farm. I mean, it must be a fantastic feeling knowing the ground you're walking on actually belongs to you!

At the top of the slope I had a check with the map – looking for landmarks. I didn't want to get lost again. I could see the grey chimneys of Hardale Hall sticking up from these dark trees, and the pub, and the church, and the river shining. It looked like a postcard, did Kirkby Haverston.

But the other way, the way I was going . . . It looked like the bones of an old tramp, with bits of brown cloth still sticking to them. A giant tramp who'd been murdered and tied down – the dry-stone walls over the fells looked just like ropes.

Still, once I started walking it was all right, even going down to Hardale. It smelt good too. Wet and brown. It wasn't like last time Mick and me had come, even though that was only a couple of days back.

I didn't go straight up the valley. Instead I walked both ways either side, on a thin green path high above the stream and the boggy ground. Looking for something . . . I'd begun to have this idea about digging a pit and putting sharp stakes in the bottom and covering it with branches, like Indians do. I hadn't even brought a trowel with me, let alone a shovel – but I wasn't in a hurry. I was planning, thinking things over.

It seemed like quite a good idea – except I'd have to find out the paths the Beast used, or get something (mostly they use goats) to tether at a stake for bait. It crossed my mind to use Betty, Chunder's new hen, but I decided against it. It would have broken his heart and, anyway, there were sheep and lambs about, weren't there?

And the other idea I was chewing over was this. It showed a cave on the map – right up the head of Hardale. And I thought maybe if the Beast was using it as a lair to sleep in during the day, I could put a net across the front, like you do across rabbit holes when you're ferreting. Of course, it would have to be a bloody big net, and I didn't know where I could get one from, except that you sometimes see lorries with rope nets over their loads instead of tarpaulins.

The last idea I had was poison. I knew where there was some – up on the allotments. Weed-killer. It's pretty lethal stuff. I'd have had to put some in a dead rabbit, or even better, in a dead sheep . . . But then I'd have to persuade the Beast to eat it. Easier said than done. Cats are right faddy about their food, you know. They don't eat anything that smells a bit suspicious or that's going bad. And I reckoned panthers would probably be the same.

About dinner time I sat on a rock and ate some bread and a Mars Bar. I was beginning to feel at home. It was like my Plan. I began to daydream about not going back to Long Moor Lane until Dad came home. No more school. No more Haverston . . . .

I'd stay up here. Spring was coming on – soon there'd be eggs about, and I could always nip down into Kirkby Haverston at night and milk that cow I'd seen in a field by the farm . . . Maybe I could live in that cave up Hardale, if the Beast wasn't using it. And, one day, I'd find the Beast injured and I'd look after it. (It would have stood on a broken bottle, maybe, or got barbed-wire tangled round it.) And it would come and live in the cave with me. We'd hunt the moors together – rabbits, hares, deer, maybe the odd sheep or two when we got desperate. And then I'd find a young kestrel, or, even better, a peregrine falcon, and rear it, and it would hunt with us – pheasant and quail (well, not with a kestrel. It would have to be a peregrine) and pigeons and grouse and duck. Even the odd starling if times were hard.

I'd call the Beast, Beast, and I'd call the falcon, Arrow, or maybe Sky Lord.

And, one time, I'd be ill (with pneumonia, I expect). It would be touch and go, but the Beast would drag me back to the cave and keep me warm with its body, and bring me water in its mouth. I'd get better, of course.

We'd roam the moors, learn the secret paths over Aggerton Moss, and we'd fight Evil. These villains would rob the bank in Haverston. I'd see it happening, because I'd have eyes like a hawk by then, and I'd have learned to run as fast as a panther. I'd cut down a tree to block the road. Then me and the Beast would tackle them, and Sky Lord would be swooping at their eyes. We wouldn't kill them or owt, just tie them up and vanish. The police would find them, raving on and on about this boy in sheep-skins, and this panther . . .

Hell, it was a good daydream. It'd make a smashing film, I reckon. I expect it would have a sad end though. Someone would shoot Sky Lord or the Beast by accident, and I'd be dragged back to civilisation . . .

Daft, eh? But I was ready to set off again after that.

It's a bleak old place, is Hardale. Even in sunshine one side of the valley is dark, in the shadow of rocks. It's a dead-end, steep sides, scree, a small black pond at the end, called Black Tarn on the map. It is black and all with the peat, and oily-looking with dead brown marsh grass growing round the edges, and bits of foam clinging round the grass, just like the froth on beer.

Bleak and silent. It's the steepness that does it, boxing the silence in.

I went very, very carefully. My eyes began to ache with looking round. I wasn't daydreaming any more, but carrying my air-rifle in my hands, and having a burning sensation in my guts, wishing it was a real gun.

I didn't go right to the head of the valley. I could see a dark crack in the rocks which I reckoned must be the cave. I didn't want to push my luck. If the Beast was asleep in there I wasn't about to go and wake him up.

I saw nothing. I mean, no dead sheep lying about – apart from a sheep skull that must have been there for years. It was weathered grey and going a bit green with mould.

It's a long walk. By the time I got back to the entrance of the valley it was full of darkness, even though the sun still hadn't gone down. By now I was feeling very jumpy, and all the warmth had gone from the afternoon. The sky was so clear you could tell it was going to freeze. Two stars were already out – like a couple of white eyes staring at me from the top of Hardale Head.

I had to decide what to do. Either I'd got to find somewhere to stay in Kirkby Haverston – or I'd have to go back home. But I didn't feel I'd got anywhere. I'd seen nothing of the Beast – not even a footprint or a scrap of dead lamb. I guessed that the best time to see it would be late at night or very early in the morning, around dawn.

I started walking back to the village – and I was walking a bit quicker than when I'd come that way first thing. I thought about sleeping in the church if they'd left it unlocked again, but when I came down into the street and saw the first lights on in the houses I got to seeing how dark and cold it had become. And I thought about our Chunder going frantic if I didn't get back . . .

I wrapped my air-rifle up in the dustbin liner I'd brought with me. I didn't want anyone to see it – because you can be done for carrying an offensive weapon – then I set off to hitch back.

Even by the time I'd come out the other end of the village and got onto the road over Aggerton Moss all the rest of the stars were out. Bright, bright stars, millions of them, and you could tell where Haverston was because there was an orangey glow over the valley at the far edge of the Moss.

A couple of cars whizzed by, but they didn't stop. My boots sounded loud on the tarmac, and the little echo of them made it sound as if someone was walking behind me. When I walked faster, the echo walked faster. When I stopped and listened, it stopped and listened. Daft, but I began to scare myself with the sound of my own blooming feet!

More cars passed. One even looked as if it was slowing down, and I ran towards it, but it drove on. I expect the bloke was looking back to see if I was a girl, and when I wasn't, he put his foot down again.

All the way back I walked. My breath was making wisps of steam, and the stars were that bright you could almost see your own shadow, even though there wasn't any moon.

Then I came down off the edge of the Moss, and there was Haverston – rows and rows of house lights glittering, and the orange street lamps snaking through, and the distant sound of traffic and the smell of soot. I'll tell you – I was glad to see it, and I jogged down to the end of Long Marsh Lane, cutting across the moor and coming in through the allotments.

And I was just thinking I'd buy some chips at Danny's, because I was starving and they smelled lovely on the cold air, when I saw the police car parked outside our house.

I shot back round the side of the houses, out of sight, panting. They'd found out about the camera! And maybe that jerk of an editor had rung them – theft, threatening behaviour, damage to property (I'd only knocked the papers off his desk, but you know what people are like for making mountains out of molehills), truancy. And Chunder would be in a hell of a temper if he'd discovered I'd nicked that fiver.

I wasn't about to walk into the middle of all that. That blue flame shot up. They weren't going to stop me! Not now! Never!

I didn't stop. I hurried back over the moor and onto the road. The church would have to do after all, and I was seething again, because I'd walked all that flaming way just to find *them* waiting. It was as if they'd deliberately planned it!

I didn't try hitching again. When I heard a car coming, I ducked down at the edge of the road, in case it was the police. But there weren't many cars by now anyway. I was in a hell of a mood, I can tell you, and it made it even worse when I heard this bus coming. I could tell it was a bus by the sound, and by the lights on it coming over the Moss. I stepped out to wave it down, but the driver didn't even slow up. I know there wasn't a regular bus stop or owt, but you'd have thought he could have sodding stopped! I ran after it, swearing at him, for all the good it did. Then I trudged on. I wasn't even listening to my footsteps any more. My ears were that full of anger and the daft kind of echo of my own swearing.

I must have been less than a mile away from Kirkby Haverston when I began to get this feeling. I'd started listening for something without really noticing that that was what I was doing. And then the hair began to creep on the back of my neck, and I did notice.

There was nothing to hear, and yet I was hearing something. I didn't slow down. I didn't stop and look round. I didn't walk any faster at first – because walking faster would have been like admitting there was something there. And now the crunch of my boots was like interference. The sounds I was listening for were so small and faint, and I couldn't tell where they were coming from.

It was like trying to stretch your ears to hear further. And then, on the rise of the road ahead, something moved against those millions of stars, like a silhouette blocking them out for less than a second.

The Beast wasn't behind me. It was ahead, between me and the village, and behind me was only five miles of empty road and all the darkness of Aggerton Moss.

I stopped dead and stared into the dark, but I couldn't see anything now, except all the humps of grass and all the tussocks either side of the road looked like things crouching. I wanted to unwrap my air-rifle, but I daren't make a sound.

There were no trees, nowhere to run to. And no sound of a car. I didn't know how fast panthers can run, but I knew it would be a bloody sight faster than me.

Then I heard the sound, softer than a real sound almost. Padding. It was hard to hear because my heart was beating that loud. Coming towards me, down the dark slope of the road.

I kept having this really stupid thought about a black cat in a coal-cellar. It's our art teacher's joke. He draws a square on the blackboard and says, "What's that a picture of?"

Groan. "A black cat in a coal cellar, Sir."

There's no way I can describe how scared I was.

And suddenly I couldn't stand still any longer. I dropped my bag and made a run for it, tearing the dustbin liner off my air-rifle. Maybe I yelled. I can't remember. I can only remember running – not back the way I'd come, but sideways, into the marsh and peat of Aggerton Moss.

I was squelching and splashing and stumbling about in the dark, trying to pull the lid off a tin of slugs in my pocket, and trying not to drop the air-rifle into the water.

And, behind me, I could hear it, softly, almost dainty, padding along on big cat feet. Even without looking, I could see the way it would spring from tussock to tussock, jump peaty streams I was wading through and half sinking up to my knees in, with the icy water making me want to scream.

And the Beast wasn't even trying. It was just loping softly along.

I didn't just think I might die – I knew I was going to. I'd never see Dad again.

I could hardly breathe, and it felt like someone had started pole-axing me in the ribs. And part of me couldn't believe any of this was happening at all.

"Chunder! Dad! Dad!" this voice was screaming. But it stopped after a while.

Then Aggerton Moss grabbed me by the legs. I'd run smack into a moss pool – like quicksand, only it's a deep hole full of sphagnum moss and wet peat. I tried to heave my legs out, sucking and squelching, round the edge. Hardly moving at all, but just moving a bit, and the coldness . . . The freezing coldness . . .

I stopped. I'd gone down up to my thighs nearly. I didn't

want to run any more – I just wanted to be dead and warm. And I couldn't run any more. Struggling was only making me sink deeper.

Then the panther came. Hardly running. It stopped at the edge of the moss pool and growled. I saw a flash of white teeth, a cloud of breath.

It sprang – more like playful than full stretch. A small jump.

I fired the air-rifle. Its bang was loud and stupid, like a kid bursting a paperbag.

The Beast was in the middle of the moss pool. It roared. But it didn't come any closer. It was sinking! Roaring, and plunging up and down, trying to drag itself out!

I could smell its breath. Warm. Beast. No. I can't describe it.

I cranked my air-rifle and fired it again – I don't know if I hit it or not, but it didn't like the noise at any rate! And it's plunging and growling and thrashing its tail. Coming closer, but sinking! Sinking! Sinking!

"Sink! Sink, yer devil!" I was screaming. I managed to crank up one more shot, then I started chucking slugs at its head. The whole pool's wallowing and I've gone down a bit further, but I'm still here and it can't bloody reach me! And all I knew was – the more it thrashed, the more it would sink.

So I'm yelling at it, and trying to load up and crank, and wanging slugs and handfuls of freezing muddy moss!

And it's roaring and snarling – and stuck! Bloody stuck!

I tried to back out, sitting down nearly and falling backwards, and still chucking slugs, and beating at the water with my air-rifle, until I could grab some grass and pull, slow as hell, slow as dying, slowly, slowly, until the weight's off my legs and I can pull meself clear!

It's like a bloody miracle! I'm dancing up and down, and yelling and howling, and shooting slug after slug almost leisurely like. I can't believe it! And this cat's screaming almost – horrible it is.

Snarling! Screaming! Thrashing about! Going on forever.

Then suddenly it's quiet. No, I mean the roaring stops. And I've stopped yelling and shooting. There's just sucking and splashing noises, and the Beast's going to die. It's going down, death in its silence, death in its struggling. The black water's shining, and the terrible earth smell of it all churned up – stinking it is. And the Beast doesn't look like a cat any more – it looks like a water monster. Humpy back, its head bony with all its fur wet. Bubbles – hardly seeing them as much as hearing them.

And then there's only the silence of Aggerton Moss. Stars. Ripples fading on the moss pool. The orangey glow of Haverston. Silence.

I didn't kill the Beast – Aggerton Moss did.

I was sick. My legs crumpled and I spewed up, retching and retching, until I just couldn't any more. And I was crying my head off.

You ask anyone at *The Cocks* what state I was in when I crawled through the pub door.

I'd lost one of my boots in the moss. I was soaked to the bone. I think now I would have died if it hadn't been for those two cars. Oh – they didn't stop. They never saw us. But I saw the headlights and I crawled in that direction. It wasn't like the films when people get up and stride away. I crawled until I got to the road. I was still clutching my air-rifle, using it like a stick and a lever.

I hardly remember getting to the village at all. Just retching up nothing but burning spit, and shaking until it felt like all my bones were going to jump out of their sockets or break.

I hardly even remember getting to the pub. Just lights. And people all talking, and someone pulling all my clothes off and shoving me in a bath. Blankets. Drinking hot whisky or brandy. And spewing up again.

Then Chunder being there, and me in a bed, croaking, "Don't turn the light off!" The Beast was dead, but I didn't want to be in the dark.

And crying. I remember Chunder's rough old hand trying to stroke me, and me crying. Very quietly. Because I was alive.

Because the Beast was dead.

# Chapter 10

They didn't believe me.

I wasn't aware of it at first – everyone at the pub was so nice and that, letting Chunder stay and not charging him or owt, getting the doctor, and making soup for me and cups of tea.

When the doctor asked what had happened, I heard the landlord, Mr Garnett, say, "Seems like the lad got lost on Aggerton Moss."

The doctor gave me some stuff for the pneumonia, because he said that was what I'd got, and if it got any worse I'd have to go into hospital. And he kept saying, "You're a lucky lad. Might have died of exposure on a night like last night."

Not a word about the Beast – though I was sure I'd said something about what had happened.

But it was good, just lying there next morning, warm and tucked up, in this lovely clean room in the pub.

Then Chunder came in to see me. You could tell he'd been worried, even though he was smiling. "Now then, our Billy, what've yer been doing to theesen? Almost give us a heart attack when old Bill turned up in his van – saying you were in a right state at the pub!"

"I'm all right now," I said. "It drowned, Chunder! It sank – I thought it was going to have me when I got stuck in that bog."

"What did, Billy?" says Chunder, quietly, sitting on the edge of the bed. "I don't follow thee, lad."

"The Beast!" I said.

He just sort of looked at me. So I tried to tell him what happened – everything, including the police car outside our house.

Chunder says, "Police never came to see me last night . . . I know there was some trouble over at Danny's. Maybe they come to sort it out? What were you fretting about coppers for, Billy?"

So then I told him everything – the camera. The lot.

He didn't say a dicky bird. He just sat frowning at me. Then he said;

"What do you fancy for breakfast?"

"What's the matter?" I says. "I'll make sure the camera gets back to Oggy – and when he hears what happened, I bet he won't do owt, Chunder."

"Aye," says Chunder. It's like a sigh. Then he went out.

I didn't go back to sleep. To tell truth, I felt baffled. I almost felt like crying again – but I didn't. There was nowt to cry over. Bits of what had happened kept flashing in my mind. Especially that silence when the Beast was drowning . . .

Mrs Garnett came up. "How are you feeling, Billy?"

"Alright. Ta."

"Good lad. You gave us all a scare – the way you came staggering in last night, love. Now, I've washed all your clothes – and when you feel a bit better Jack'll run you and Chunder home. You'll be better in your own bed. Here you are, you drink this tea up. I've put two sugars in."

She was really nice – smiling and fussing about the bed.

"I don't suppose they'll be able to dredge it up," I said, more to myself than to her.

"What's that, Billy?"

"The Beast, out of the moss pool . . . It'd be really great to have its head on our living-room wall when Dad gets back!"

She gave me a funny look. "Aye. You were muttering something like that – Beast and that – when I bathed you."

"You bathed me!" I felt a bit hot.

"You've got nothing I haven't seen before, love," says Mrs Garnett, laughing. "I've got two lads of my own, you know." And she went off downstairs.

Later, Chunder came back.

I said to him about dredging the Beast up and having its head put on our wall – and I wanted that Mr Arkwright to see it.

Chunder shook his head. He said, "Listen, lad. I don't know what happened last night . . . Sounds like you give yourself a real fright . . . "

"What? What do you mean?"

Chunder breathed in, then he says, "Josh Lacey shot that dog the day before yesterday – a Doberman. It was chasing a ewe – it'd already killed one lamb when he saw what was going on. Josh Lacey killed the Haverston Beast, Billy. Day before yesterday."

I sat up. It was like being knifed in the ribs. I was staring at him.

"It wasn't a flaming dog! Chunder, I'm telling you! Get them to drag that pool! It was a panther! It chased me, Grandad! I saw it!"

"Of course you did, lad," says Chunder, in that voice you use to little kids. That voice you use when you don't believe them and you don't want to hurt their feelings.

No one believed me. I bet you don't believe me even.

The sheep killing stopped, and the *Haverston Gazette* had a picture of Josh Lacey on the front page. REIGN OF TERROR ENDS, it said. The business man gave him the five hundred pounds, and some other folks sent him cheques and postal-orders to help pay for the damage done to his flock and to the other farmers' flocks.

I lay in bed. I couldn't believe it. I lay there and everyone thought I was lying through my teeth – or that I was delirious with the pneumonia. Of course all the flaming sheep killing stopped! The Beast was lying under half a ton of peat and water and moss. No one would even go and look!

HAVERSTON BEAST'S LAST VICTIM – it wasn't even on the front page the week after. It was that old widow from Crag Cottage. The Buddhist one – found dead in a patch of brambles and bushes by a wall near Kirkby Haverston. Cause of death, the coroner said, was a fractured skull received in a fall. She'd fallen backwards and cracked her head on a rock. And her left arm was almost eaten off.

I knew where that wall was. She'd been dead three weeks. I'd heard the Beast crunching the bones of that poor old woman's arm – and so had Mick . . .

But it was no good . . . It was like going mental, lying there. Even Mick Dalton didn't believe me. Mick! Who'd seen the Beast! He said he did, but he didn't.

I kept saying to Chunder – why don't you ask the police to find that circus? Someone knew that panther had escaped – or they had let it out when the police came round, because they panicked, not having a licence to keep it. But he wouldn't.

After two weeks, I stopped talking about it. It was easier. I didn't want people laughing – saying I was like Jim Dalton.

I told Chunder that I'd tell my dad about it when he got home. That was a few days after I'd got up. I felt all right – the pain had gone from my chest. Inside my head I felt . . . I felt . . . Nothing. Numb.

But Chunder said, "Billy, I tried to tell you, but you wouldn't listen. Your Dad's in prison, lad. He got into a fight in Glasgow – lost his rag and hit a copper. They gave him two years. But don't you worry – he'll be out sooner than that."

Nothing.

Numb.


Then comes the first day back at school.

I didn't get there till dinner time. I sneaked in, looking for Oggy. He'd believe me – and I wanted to explain about the camera. Mick had been made to give it back. The police had been round to his house and got it off him. He was going to be charged, and so was I. Mick said Oggy didn't want to press charges, but the Head had made him, to set an example.

It was quiet in the corridors. Everyone was outside for dinner break.

I went to our classroom.

There were voices. Oggy and a woman. So I waited outside, not wanting to see him when there was anyone else about.

"I'm sorry," she said, "But I can't see any way round it. I called at the house when the boy was ill. The grandfather had obviously been drinking. There were bird-droppings on the kitchen floor, and the place obviously hadn't been cleaned for weeks. I went up and looked in the boy's bedroom. He was asleep under one thin blanket and a coat. It was bitterly cold in there! For God's sake, the child was suffering from pneumonia! There wasn't even a light bulb in his room, let alone a radiator!

"I gather that the father is in prison for assaulting a police officer, and as for the mother – she abandoned the family after William Coward's birth.

"I'm sorry, but it seems to me, I've no alternative. I'll press for a care order. It's my hope that foster parents can be found for the boy. If not, there's always Ridge Hill."

*Blue flames. Blue cold flames. The freezing coldness . . . Stars. Silence. And the rippling ring of black water. A blue flame.*

"No, I'm sorry!" Oggy said. "It seems to me you haven't begun to understand what I was telling you. Take that lad away from his grandfather and you'll break his heart! You'll break both their hearts! They're *survivors* – can't you understand that? That lad went hunting the Haverston Beast with an air-rifle – at least, that's what he believed he was doing! He would have known an air-rifle was ineffectual against a dog – but he went all the same!"

"I'm sorry, Mr Oglethorpe, that's totally beside the point.

It's simply no use being sentimental in a case like this. This boy needs caring for. The case is before the magistrates next Tuesday. Michael Dalton should get off with a fine. But William Coward needs more than that. He needs help. I've told you what I shall be recommending, and I'm afraid nothing you've said has altered my opinion . . . "

I ran.

The Haverston Beast is dead. I saw him die. I wish he was still alive. I wish he'd come padding along High Street!

The Haverston Beast is dead, or so they think.

I'll not be there next Tuesday.

I've got my air-rifle. I've packed a bag. If they want me, they'll have to come and get me. They'll have to hunt me down.

Don't tell them, but I'm going up Hardale. The Haverston Beast is dead.

They've not seen nothing yet.

I'm going to take over where the Beast left off.

They've not seen nothing yet!